# Doomed Queen Anne

# Doomed Queen Anne

A Young Royals Book

Carolyn Meyer

SCHOLASTIC INC.
New York Toronto London Auckland Sydney
Mexico City New Delhi Hong Kong Buenos Aires

*Doomed Queen Anne* is a work of fiction based on historical figures and events. Some details have been altered to enhance the story.



ISBN 0-439-55955-3


Published by Scholastic Inc., 557 Broadway, New York, NY 10012, by arrangement with Harcourt, Inc. 

12 11 10 9 8 7 6 13 14 15 16 17 18 19 20

Printed in the U.S.A. 40

First Scholastic printing, September 2003

Text set in Bembo

Designed by Lydia D'moch

*For Sophie,*
*the newest princess*

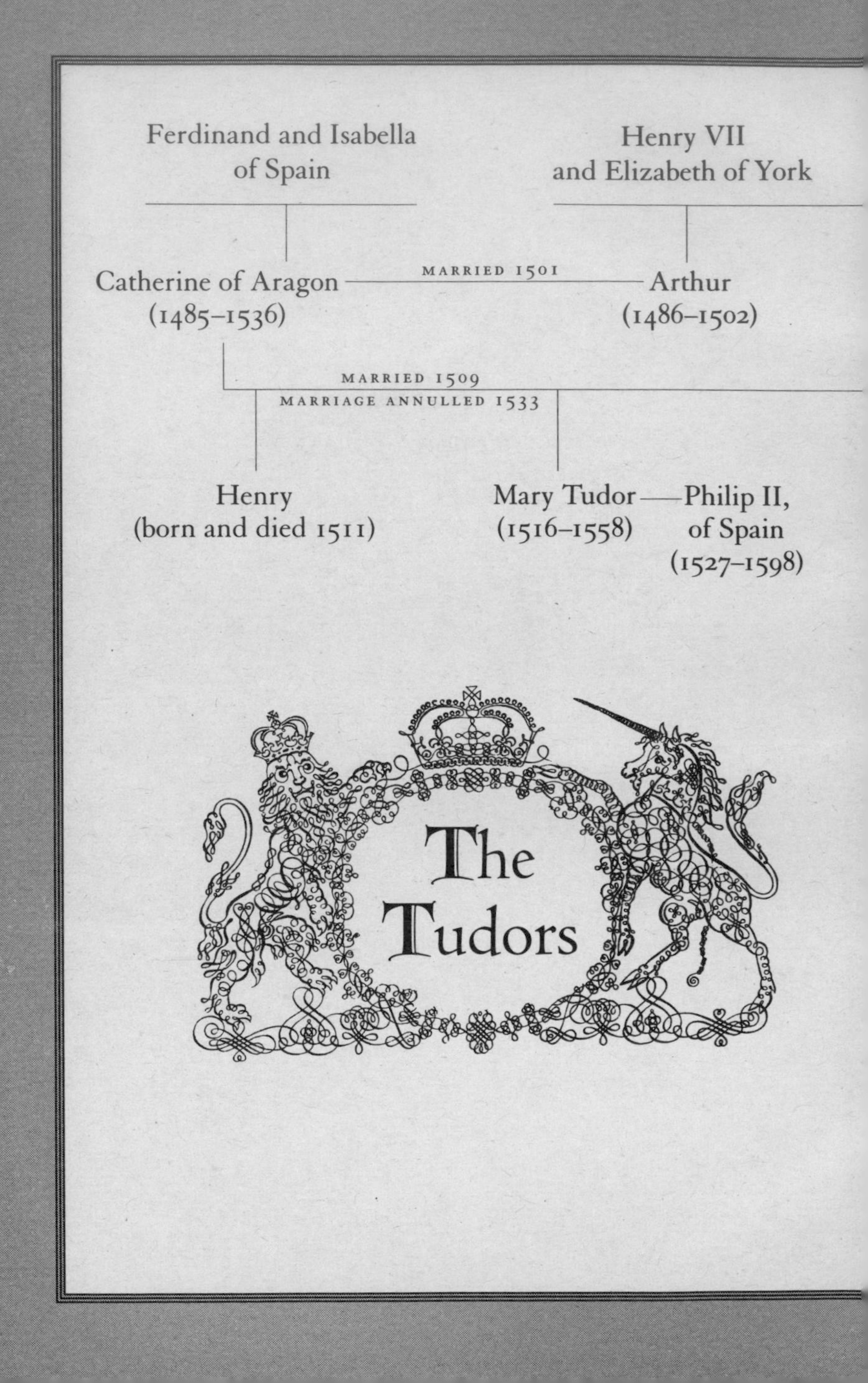
Ferdinand and Isabella
of Spain
Henry VII
and Elizabeth of York
Catherine of Aragon
(1485–1536)
MARRIED 1501
Arthur
(1486–1502)
MARRIED 1509
MARRIAGE ANNULLED 1533
Henry
(born and died 1511)
Mary Tudor
(1516–1558)
Philip II,
of Spain
(1527–1598)
The
Tudors

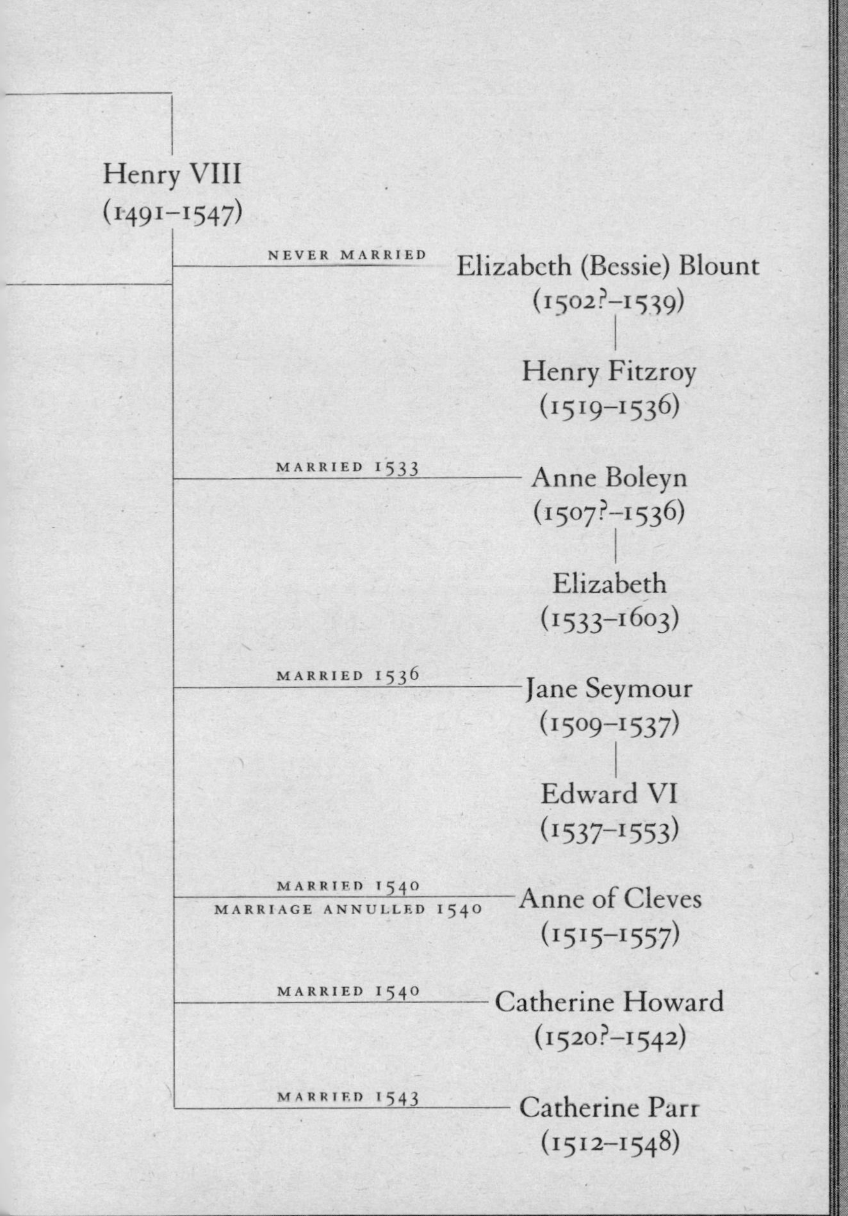
Henry VIII
(1491–1547)
NEVER MARRIED
Elizabeth (Bessie) Blount
(1502?–1539)
Henry Fitzroy
(1519–1536)
MARRIED 1533
Anne Boleyn
(1507?–1536)
Elizabeth
(1533–1603)
MARRIED 1536
Jane Seymour
(1509–1537)
Edward VI
(1537–1553)
MARRIED 1540
MARRIAGE ANNULLED 1540
Anne of Cleves
(1515–1557)
MARRIED 1540
Catherine Howard
(1520?–1542)
MARRIED 1543
Catherine Parr
(1512–1548)

# *PROLOGUE*

## *The Tower of London, England*
## *19 May 1536*

Midnight. Darkness, but for this single candle. By first light I must be ready. I am very afraid; my hands tremble, and my throat aches with stifled sobs.

Silence, save for the wheezes of Sir William Kingston, the constable of the Tower, and his wife, who sleep outside my door. The ladies assigned to watch over me toss restlessly on pallets on the floor.

I shall not sleep. I sit now in the chambers prepared these three years past by King Henry for my coronation. My gown is ready, gray silk damask opening upon a petticoat of white silk. Over it I shall wear my crimson velvet mantle trimmed in ermine—a queen's robe—and I shall put my hair up in a net of gold.

For the next hours I have little to do but to pray and to remember the events of my life and the people who brought me to this place: King Henry, whose ardor turned to hatred. My father, who encouraged my ambition but hardened against me when I learned my lessons too well. My sister, whom I envied above all others. My brother, who was condemned to die because of me.

And my child—what will become of her? Will she be told that her mother was once queen of England? Or will her father try to erase all remembrance of me? If I could be granted but one wish (other than the wish for life itself) it would be that my daughter know the truth about me—Anne Boleyn, the doomed queen.

CHAPTER 1

# The Grand Rendezvous

## 1520

Somewhere in that enormous throng was my hateful sister, and I resolved to find her.

It had been three years since Mary went home to England. Now she'd come back to France, and I wished to show her how much I had changed. She would see that I was no longer the ill-favored child she'd once taunted. I was now a fine young lady of the court! But first I had to find her.

Permission to go in search of my sister would never have been granted by the mother of the maids, the squint-eyed Madame Mathilde, and so I determined to go without asking. I dressed in one of my prettiest gowns and restlessly awaited my chance to slip away.

The moment Madame Mathilde was distracted, I gathered my courage and my skirts and hurried out of the French royal encampment. Plunging into the noisy tumult, I was swept up in the colorful jostling of lords and ladies, knights and priests, tradesmen and servants, horses and dogs. Surely, with such a crowd, my absence would not be noticed. Then I saw a one-eyed man watching me. Had he been set to spying by the mother of the maids? His look chilled me, and with racing heart I ran toward the English camp.

I had just passed my thirteenth birthday in June of the year 1520 and was part of the great entourage that accompanied François, king of France, to meet with Henry VIII, king of England. The entire French court had made the five-day journey north from Paris and King Henry and *his* great entourage—including my sister—had sailed across the English Channel so that the two powerful rulers could pledge their mutual friendship. Their grand rendezvous was to be an event of unrivaled splendor. Thousands of artisans and workmen had labored for months to transform this dusty plain into two royal encampments. Hundreds of tents fashioned of cloth of gold and silk in brilliant colors shimmered in the late afternoon sun. No wonder it was called the Field of Cloth of Gold.

What excitement! Butchers hurried by with hogs suspended from poles; bakers carried great wooden trays stacked high with manchets made of the finest wheaten flour. Musicians played upon their pipes, and I stopped to watch a trained bear dance while his master drummed. But then I thought I saw the one-eyed man again, and I hurried on.

Once I reached the English camp, hardly anyone took notice of me, a small, dark-haired girl, asking for Lady Mary Bullen or Marie Boleyn (our father had changed the spelling of our family name from *Bullen* to the more fashionably French-sounding *Boleyn*). Everyone seemed to know who she was. She had once been a blazing star in the French court, and it was no surprise that she had managed to attract the same sort of attention in England as well. I was directed to a sumptuous tent of yellow silk. Suddenly I felt uneasy. How would my sister receive me? What if she laughed at me! Cautiously I pushed aside the curtain and peered inside.

My sister rested upon an embroidered pillow, sipping from a silver goblet. She was full-breasted and narrow-waisted, her hair as thick and rich as honey, her fair complexion touched with pink, her eyes the color of spring violets. Her brows were delicately arched, her rosy lips pleasingly bow shaped. She shone with the special radiance of one well pleased with herself.

The moment I found her, I regretted it. The refinements I had acquired—the elegant wardrobe, the refined manners, the excellent French, the graceful dancing—all meant nothing. My sister had become a great beauty, and I knew at once that I was still the ill-favored child.

At the sight of me, she set down the goblet. "Dear sister!" she cried, and rose gracefully to greet me before I could change my mind and flee. We embraced, as was expected, although I felt no real affection from her, and I caught a whiff of her scent.

She held me at arm's length and inspected me with a critical eye, taking in my long, dark hair; my dark eyes, nearly black; my skin white as skimmed milk, with no hint of blush; my newly budded breasts. Then she reached out to examine the jewel I wore close around my neck on a bit of ribbon, intended to conceal a large mole that grew at the base of my throat. I thought the disguise effective, but Mary managed to move the jewel in such a way that I was sure called attention to the flaw. "How clever," she said.

Scorched by her critical gaze, I pulled away from her and adjusted the jewel.

"You look much too thin, Nan," my sister said. "Are you well?"

"Quite well," I replied. My sister had always been the first to notice my faults, and that had not changed. And she had forgotten her promise to call me Anne instead of my childhood name of Nan. All of my confidence seemed to drain away, and I did not correct her.

Mary bade me sit down near her. A serving maid brought me a goblet of the spiced wine that poured from one of the many gilded fountains. "Have you heard the gossip?" Mary asked before I could ask after our parents and brother. She pursed her pretty red lips and tossed her curls.

"I hear gossip every day," I replied carefully, wondering what she intended. "One cannot be a member of the royal court and *not* hear gossip. Of what do you speak, dear sister?"

She called for her servant to bring a tray of sweetmeats, and when we had each selected one and Mary had taken a dainty bite, she leaned toward me with a coy smile. "I am the king's mistress."

I gaped at her. "The king?" I repeated, rather stupidly. "King Henry?"

"Of course, King Henry!" she said, laughing. "Of what other king would I speak? It is quite an honor to be chosen by one's monarch."

"I assume that your King Henry has several mistresses," I replied, annoyed by her boasting and determined not to let her best me. "François certainly does." This was not an exaggeration; everyone knew that the king of France was in love with the comtesse de Châteaubriant, and that he enjoyed the favors of many other women as well.

"The king does as the king wishes," Mary informed me with a shrug. "And I care not with whom he does it when he is not in my company. But I assure you that he has long since tired of Queen Catherine. And he no longer pays the least attention to his former mistress, Bessie Blount. He has given me this gown," she said, flaunting her velvet sleeves and a brocade petticoat.

My sister was gotten up in the English fashion: a gown with too many colors, too much gold lace and brocade, too much of everything. I preferred the refined elegance of the way we dressed in the French court.

"And this ring as well," she added. She waved the bauble under my nose. It was gold, set with rubies and diamonds.

Mary could not stop prating about King Henry. "He had a child by Bessie about a year ago, before he tired of her and sent her away. Henry Fitzroy is the little one's name, and being the king's son, he is treated with all manner of deference, even though he is a bastard. When we are alone, the king talks constantly of how keenly he desires a son to inherit the throne."

"King Henry has a daughter, has he not?" I asked.

"Yes, the princess Mary, poor little snip of a child." Mary sighed and sipped her wine. "The king pays her great attention—when he thinks about her!—but she is of no use to him, for she cannot rule. He must have a son—a *legitimate* son of a lawful wife, not a bastard like Bessie's Fitzroy."

"Does Queen Catherine know that you are the king's mistress?" I asked my sister.

The question caused her great merriment. "Oh, indeed she does, and she hates me! But there is nothing she can do, because I am a member of her court at the king's bidding—Father saw to that. I think Father knew that the king would come to desire me, and our affair will greatly advance Father's political position."

*Had Father really planned it all?* I wondered. *Does he have plans for me?* But I knew the answer: *I am the ill-favored daughter. He intends no such future for me.*

"Perhaps she will yet provide a son," I said, mainly to provoke my sister.

"Eleven years of marriage, and Queen Catherine has still not produced an heir for the king," Mary said scornfully. "Have you not seen her? She is short and stout, and her gowns are stiff and ugly. After all those years since she left Spain, she still cannot speak our language properly. Everything that comes out of the queen's mouth sounds Spanish! She is not at all happy that her husband takes his pleasure with me. But who could take pleasure with such an old Spanish mule? She is nearly as lacking in beauty as your pious queen Claude!" Mary laughed, and gestured for the serving maid to refill our goblets. "Claude is blessed with virtue, but virtue is a poor substitute for beauty and wit."

"Our pious queen Claude has already borne François two sons as well as a daughter and expects a fourth child in a few weeks," I retorted, still hoping to put my sister in her place. "There is no question of who will inherit the throne of France."

Just then we heard a flourish of trumpets, loud and long. "The kings are coming!" Mary cried, rising quickly from her cushion, her cheeks flushing prettily.

I hurried to follow my comely blond sister out of the silk tent to watch as the splendid royal procession approached. All around us the air seemed to crackle with excitement. I was thrilled to be a part of it, and for a time I forgot my jealousy.

"I believe they are on their way to a joust," said Mary. "Shall we hurry to the tiltyard to watch them?"

"We should be with our retinues, should we not?" I asked, suddenly worried that Madame Mathilde had taken a count of the queen's maids and found one missing.

"We can join them after the kings have passed by," she said. "But first I want to show you something. Come with me. Hurry!"

Seizing my hand, Mary pushed her way through the crowd. I stumbled after her until we reached the very front of the throng. We were close enough to touch the horses of the henchmen riding at the head of the procession, followed by the archers and the knights, all wearing brilliantly colored livery. The horses' hooves raised clouds of dust, and the air smelled strongly of their sweat and dung.

The kings rode side by side; François astride a gray courser and Henry mounted upon a huge white warhorse. The horses were trapped to the ground in crimson damask, their saddles gilded, their tack inlaid with gems. As they drew abreast of us, my sister pressed dangerously close and reached up to King Henry, offering him her handkerchief. He reined in his horse for a brief moment, accepted the bit of lace and linen and touched it to his lips, and then, smiling, plucked a jewel from his doublet and tossed it to her.

As he turned away and rode on, King Henry's gaze passed over me as though I didn't exist. I stared after this dazzling figure, unable to tear my eyes or my thoughts away from him.

"You see?" Mary crowed, showing me the pearl the king had given her. "Look for yourself how His Majesty delights in me!"

I could see, indeed. *I will never be beautiful like my sister. No king will ever want* me *for his lover.* I tried not to care, and I tried not to show how much I *did* care. But I began to wonder if there was a way I might best my sister and achieve more than she had even dreamed of. What a triumph *that* would be!

If Mary noticed my darkening mood, she gave no sign as we hurried toward the lists. We should have been with our retinues to make a formal entrance: Mary with Queen Catherine and I with Queen Claude. We would surely be chastised for our tardiness. But Mary didn't seem concerned, and suddenly neither was I. It was worth whatever punishment I would receive to have been so close to the king of England.

I STILL REMEMBER the first time I set eyes upon King Henry VIII. When I was four years old, my parents left my little brother, George, behind at our castle at Hever, in Kent, and journeyed with my sister and me to the royal palace in Greenwich for the Yuletide celebration. Mary, who was then nine, had visited court before. Naturally, she had a pretty new gown, pale green silk over a yellow petticoat, and I was given one of her outgrown gowns, but I was too excited to mind very much. For weeks our governess, Lady Guildford, had rehearsed me in court behavior.

"Whenever the king and queen enter the hall or leave it, everyone must rise. The gentlemen bow low, and the ladies drop into a deep curtsy. Like this." She demonstrated, holding out her skirts, inclining her head, and gracefully bending her knees. I copied her until she was satisfied.

At last we stood in the crowd that had gathered at Greenwich to greet the arrival of the king and queen from London. Trumpets heralded their approach, and I strained for a glimpse of the royal couple. Queen Catherine rode in a fine litter all covered in velvet and cloth of gold, and at her side, mounted on a great black stallion, was the most magnificent man I had ever seen. He was young and handsome with red-gold hair, and he wore a dazzling cloak trimmed in ermine and covered with sparkling jewels. The crowd cheered wildly, men tossed their caps into the air, and the king and queen acknowledged our greetings with waves and smiles. The procession passed by, and the splendid king was gone long before I'd had my fill of gazing at him.

"When shall I see the king again, Father?" I asked, tugging at his sleeve. "Will he speak to me then?"

"You will see King Henry at the banquet tonight, Nan," he said. "But he will not speak to you. Hundreds will be present."

I was disappointed, but I consoled myself with the notion that I would be able to stare at him as much as I pleased.

Hours later, the hundreds of whom my father spoke assembled in the Great Hall of Greenwich Palace. There was much noise and hubbub until, from the balcony above us, a resounding trumpet fanfare hushed the crowd. As my governess had promised, the gentlemen bowed low and the ladies dropped into deep curtsies—all of the ladies, that is, but me. I was too awestruck to remember what I was to do; moreover, if I had gone down in a curtsy, I would not have been able to see the king. And so I alone remained bolt upright as King Henry and Queen Catherine entered the hall. Wanting him to notice me, I raised my hand and waved as the king's keen blue eyes swept over the crowd. The king, laughing, waved in return.

My father observed my behavior and immediately pulled me down. Later, I was birched for it—Lady Guildford administered a half dozen whacks to the backs of my legs—but I never forgot that moment when the king's eyes met mine in the midst of the crowd.

"I SHALL NO DOUBT be betrothed before Michaelmas," Mary was saying now in a matter-of-fact way that caught me off guard. We spoke French, so as not to be understood by the English ladies all around us. She was still admiring her pretty new jewel. "The king has chosen a husband for me." She said this as though it were the most common of occurrences.

"You are to be wed? To whom?" I asked, forgetting the need for haste.

"Will Carey, one of the king's courtiers. I know him well. It should be a decent match. I have no complaints about it. One husband is just as good, or bad, as the next, in my opinion."

"So that puts an end to your career as king's mistress," I said rather coldly, for I felt then that she did not deserve the special attention of "the greatest king England has ever known," as my father referred to him, adding, "or indeed shall ever know."

"Not at all!" Mary replied with spirit. "I shall continue to be the king's pleasure, if he wishes it."

"But what of your husband?" I asked, thinking, *My sister is shameless!* "Will he not object?"

She laughed. "One does not object to the desires of one's king! Of course, if I beget a child, that will put an end to it."

"Then the king will be in search of someone to

take your place, will he not?" I couldn't help asking. We had arrived at the lists where the tournaments were held, and we prepared to hurry off to join our queens, hoping to slip unnoticed among their ladies.

Mary shrugged. "No doubt. King Henry always finds his pleasure among the queen's ladies. It does put Her Majesty in a temper." My sister winked at me knowingly. "Come home to England when you tire of those overrefined Frenchmen," she said archly. "Perhaps, when you are grown up, King Henry's fancy will alight upon you. Would you not like to be the king's mistress?"

"No, I would not," I said haughtily. "Anyone can be the king's mistress. I should much prefer to be his queen."

Mary laughed, showing her perfect white teeth. "What an amusing child you have become!" she cried.

"I am not a child, and I am quite serious," I declared firmly. "Wait and see—someday I shall be queen of England, and you will kneel at my feet!" And I flounced proudly away from my well-favored, detestable sister.

CHAPTER 2

# Childhood

## 1507–1520

I was always jealous of my sister. My mother had been a great beauty, and it was evident that Mary, who favored her, would be a beauty as well. I was a severe disappointment to my parents, for I was not a comely child. I had inherited the dark looks of my father, Thomas Bullen. My mother, Elizabeth, highborn daughter of the duke of Norfolk, was a lady-in-waiting to Queen Catherine. My father lacked both title and wealth, but he was intelligent and ambitious. He meant to make himself important in the court of the brilliant young king Henry VIII. Mary and I became part of his scheme.

Soon after that long-ago visit to court, at which I

had failed to curtsy, my father decided that Mary would be sent to Paris to join the court of Louis XII, king of France. Because of the close alliance between Louis and King Henry, my father believed it would benefit him and his family to have a daughter fluent in the language and the ways of the French court.

But he had not yet decided what to do with me.

One night when we were thought to be asleep in our bed, the candles already snuffed, Mary decided that we must go to our mother for something, I forget just what. Obediently I stumbled out of bed and followed her. We crept past our governess and the serving maids, fast asleep on their pallets, pushed open the heavy oaken door carefully so the creaking iron hinges wouldn't give us away, and raced through the cold echoing hall to our mother's chambers. About to enter, we were stopped by our father's low rumbling voice within. We hushed each other and, shivering, crowded close to the keyhole to listen.

"What of Nan?" I heard my mother ask plaintively. "I cannot imagine that we shall ever be able to find her a suitable husband. The poor child is so ill-favored! Dark as a gypsy, and that blemish upon her neck, the little bud of an extra finger..."

"Ill-favored, true enough, but not dull-witted," my father replied. "I find Nan's intelligence far superior to Mary's."

*Ha!* I could not resist administering a sharp pinch to my sister through the thin silk of her sleeping shift.

She swatted my hand away, and, in the brief exchange of slaps and counterslaps that ensued, we nearly missed what was said next.

"...to a nunnery," I heard my mother say. "As other parents have done with daughters with unfortunate defects. She would avoid the miseries of childbearing. Perhaps Nan would not mind a life of prayer and stitchery," my mother continued in her placid voice.

I gasped. *Defects! A nunnery!* Mary giggled and gave me a painful blow with her elbow, but I was too horrified by what I was hearing to pay her any attention. Tears gathered in my eyes as my mother in a few words sentenced me to a life of wretched piety.

"I have a better plan, one that I have already set in motion," my father announced. "I have petitioned the king, who has agreed that Nan be sent to join the court of Archduchess Margaret in the Spanish Netherlands. Her court is said to be brilliant. Nan can learn the necessary courtly skills there, and with luck we might contract a good marriage for her with some Spanish or Italian nobleman."

Mary stared at me with her great blue eyes. Suddenly our father's footsteps approached the closed door. Fearing that we might be discovered and forgetting whatever it was we'd wanted of our mother, we raced recklessly back to our own bedchamber, shut the bed-curtains, and burrowed under the coverlet. My heart was pounding, and I felt like weeping.

"So," Mary whispered in the darkness, "you

need not go into a convent after all. Father thinks it possible to make a lady of you, even if you *are* ill-favored."

Of course I hated my sister, the cherished beauty of the family, but I took some comfort in my father's words: *She is not dull-witted.* Perhaps he would one day take pride in me after all.

I HAD NO IDEA who the Archduchess Margaret might be or where the Spanish Netherlands were. I understood only that I was to be sent far away from Hever, where I had spent my childhood. I could speak of my fears to no one—certainly not my parents, for that would have meant admitting that I had eavesdropped. Nor could I confide in my disdainful sister, who was already preparing to leave for the French court and missed no chance to lord it over me. So I kept my peace, attended to my lessons with Lady Guildford, and awaited my fate with a sinking heart.

Finally, in the autumn of 1513 when I was six, my father decided the time had come for me to leave England. Mary had sailed for France months earlier, an expensive array of new gowns and petticoats packed in her wooden trunks. Her outgrown wardrobe had been altered to fit me.

I bade my mother farewell at Hever, both of us choking back tears. I clung for a long moment to my younger brother, George, who was too young to understand that years might pass before we saw one another again. It was very hard for me to leave them.

My father had arranged for me to travel in the company of Lady Guildford, whom I neither liked nor disliked but who was at least familiar to me. Father accompanied us as far as Dover, to the small sailing ship that was to take us across the English Channel. I knelt to receive his blessing and promised that I would be a dutiful and obedient child. As soon as I was free, I hurried aboard to inspect the masts and ropes and other nautical things. I was excited, for I had never been at sea.

As the shore slipped away, billowing clouds darkened and piled one upon another; waves slapped hard at the sides of the wooden craft. No sooner were we out of sight of land than the furious storm broke from an angry sky. Hour after hour we were tossed about by cruel seas and lashed with torrential rain.

Belowdecks, bilious passengers lay strewn about; I stayed above, clinging to the mast as the ship climbed to the crest of each towering wave and then plunged into a deep trough. With the wind tearing at my sodden clothes and my streaming hair plastered to my body, I was frightened, but also exhilarated. It did not occur to me that I might die.

At last the storm subsided. As we went ashore at Calais, the captain patted me on the head and said what a brave child I was.

"Brave and foolish," Lady Guildford retorted. "It will be the death of her."

But I was not feeling at all brave as we neared the end of the three-day journey from Calais to Mechelen, capital of the Netherlands. What would the archduchess be like? Would she treat me with kindness or cruelty?

The Archduchess Margaret herself greeted us warmly at the gates of the magnificent palace, addressing me as Mademoiselle Anne. A tall woman dressed in black with shrewd eyes, she was known as Margaret of Austria or Marguerite d'Autriche, but everyone called her simply "Madame." I liked her at once.

I was still too young to become officially *une fille d'honneur,* a maid of honor. "But, Mademoiselle Anne," said Madame, "you are not too young to begin learning those things that will one day win you a favored place at any court in the world." Slowly she set my heart at ease.

I had my lessons from a tutor, Monsieur Symonnet, who spoke to me only in French, even when I wept piteously, "Oh please, monsieur, just tell me it in English!" To no avail. He merely smiled and repeated what he had just said, still in French. Gradually the sounds soaked into my mind, and my tongue learned to pronounce them.

My dancing tutor, Monsieur Bosc, was tall and thin with a wispy yellowish beard and a crooked nose. Each afternoon he arrived with his long stick for tapping out the meter. We practiced the *basse danse,* consisting of small, gliding steps, with frequent bows, followed by the leaps of the galliard, and on to the stately but complicated pavane.

"One learns to move tranquilly, without agitation," Monsieur Bosc had to remind me often, for I tended toward too much enthusiasm.

Soon after I arrived, Madame ordered new gowns and petticoats for me to replace my sister's discarded wardrobe and assigned Madame Louise, a *dame d'honneur,* to teach me the secrets of dressing well. "You will permit me to make a suggestion?" inquired Madame Louise. "If you were to wear a jewel on a ribbon around your neck, like so, it would serve to disguise the small blemish there that causes you so much displeasure." My sister had tormented me about that mole for as long as I could remember, and I welcomed Madame Louise's suggestion. "Your hands are very graceful, Mademoiselle Anne," she continued. "Perhaps a sleeve with a frilled lace cuff would enhance them and draw attention away from your finger." This, too, I welcomed.

"Men will look into your eyes and listen to your clever words," Madame Louise assured me. "You will enchant them with your whole being, and they will be blind to your little flaws. They may even come to admire them, to find them attractive."

Slowly I came to believe her.

Madame Louise herself was not a handsome woman; her nose was large and her skin pockmarked, and yet I could see for myself the powerful attraction she exercised over the gentlemen in Archduchess Margaret's court. They seemed to find her ravishing.

I HAD BEEN WITH Archduchess Margaret for nearly a year when I received a summons from my father. I was to move to Paris with Lady Guildford. I burst into tears at the news. I did not want to leave the archduchess, whom I'd come to love, and this place where I had learned to be happy. Of course, I had no choice. I had to obey.

The reason for the change was this: Princess Mary, the younger sister of King Henry VIII, was to be married to King Louis XII of France. My father had been chosen to accompany the princess and her large retinue to Paris. I was to join him and my sister there. With the blessings of the archduchess and many last instructions from Madame Louise, I made my tearful farewells and was on my way to a new life in the French court. Naturally, I worried about how I would get on with my sister.

I was seven years old, but not at all the same child who'd left England more than a year earlier. I no longer wore clumsy English gowns or displayed clumsy English manners. I was becoming a *demoiselle,* which was obvious even to my sister.

"You have changed, Nan," she said the first time we met, looking at me with narrowed eyes. My sister was twelve and now called Marie, but in some ways—ways that surely did not escape her notice—I seemed nearly as sophisticated as she.

Marie linked her arm through mine as we strolled in the palace gardens. "Poor Princess Mary!" she whispered. "She despises King Louis. He is old and feeble, but Henry is forcing her to marry him. What is more, she is in love with someone else—King Henry's friend, Charles Brandon. That is a secret, of course."

"Pity," I said, although frankly I did not care how the princess felt about her betrothed. We were all taught from an early age that marriage had nothing to do with the feelings of the bride or bridegroom. For royalty, marriage was about political alliances, just as, for those of us of lesser status, marriage was about wealth and property and rank. Of course, I knew nothing about love.

Princess Mary was a lovely creature with red-gold hair and merry blue eyes, eighteen years old and full of life. King Louis had scarcely a tooth left in his mouth; a servingman hovered at his elbow to wipe the tears from his weeping eyes and spittle from his drooling lips. *No wonder the princess doesn't want to marry him,* I thought, and I did feel sorry for her.

For the next few weeks, I was kept busy helping Marie, who was supposed to translate for the wedding guests who spoke English or French but rarely both. The difficulty was that my sister, however fluent she may have thought herself, spoke clumsy French. My French was now excellent, and often I was called upon to untangle her misinterpretations.

"You have become impossible, Nan," she said spitefully. "Just because you think you know French!"

"But I *do* know French, dear sister," I gloated. Aware that she was waiting for the first opportunity to pinch me, I managed to stay just beyond her reach.

The wedding took place in October. Three weeks later Princess Mary was crowned Queen Mary of France; more pageantry, more feasting, more dancing. The young queen was always polite and attentive to the pitiable old king. At the great Yuletide feast, Queen Mary herself helped the wretched man totter to the banqueting table.

By then, Marie was scarcely speaking to me. She realized that I had learned to dance better than she could, and she resented my attempts to teach her the steps. Our new relationship angered her. "Since you have come here, everyone watches you, and I have been forgotten!" she complained pettishly.

"I am sure that you are mistaken," I said, but I knew that she was right. That pleased me a great deal.

Once she slapped me, and I responded by pulling her hair. Marie screamed, and several maids of honor rushed to separate us. The mother of the maids punished us both, sending us to our chambers without bread or wine, where we sulked and blamed each other. But in the end I proved the stronger, or perhaps the more stubborn, of the two, and it was Marie who gave in.

"Forgive me, Nan," she said. "Let us be friends, for in truth we have only each other."

I pretended to consider that. "We shall be friends and sisters," I said at last, "but you must promise never to call me Nan. My name is now Anne."

She did, and we kissed each other and made up.

Then on New Year's Day the drooling old king fell dead. Our lovely queen Mary was now a widow. She had been married only eighty-two days, and it is my belief that she was still a virgin.

"Now she is free to marry Brandon," my sister whispered to me as we prepared for the funeral. "Before she married Louis, she made King Henry agree that she could marry whomever she likes after Louis died."

My sister was right. King Henry sent his courtier Charles Brandon to Paris to fetch the widow and as much of her dowry as could be reclaimed. Instead, Charles and Mary were wed in secret! When King Henry found out about it, he was furious.

"Why is the king so angry?" I asked. "Had he not promised that she could wed whom she pleased? Is Brandon not his friend?"

"Perhaps King Henry never intended to keep his word," said Marie. "But he is especially angry because Queen Mary married beneath her, and without his permission. He claims that Brandon betrayed him. Now they will have to apply to the king's chancellor, Cardinal Wolsey, to secure forgiveness."

How could she know all this? Only five years older than I, Marie seemed to understand exactly how the court operated, even if she could not remember the steps of the pavane and her French was an embarrassment.

But none of this mattered very much, except to Queen Mary and Charles Brandon, because soon a new king of France was crowned. François le Premier (Francis I, in English) was married to the dead king's daughter, Claude, who was just fifteen. Instead of returning to the court of Archduchess Margaret or to England with Mary and Charles Brandon, I was invited to remain in Paris in the court of Queen Claude.

And so was Marie. Thus began the next chapter of my education, with my sister as my tutor.

THE NEW FRENCH KING was tall and well made and good-humored as well. François loved having beautiful ladies around him. Often I heard him say, "A court without women is a year without spring and a spring without roses." Queen Claude, on the other hand, was noted for her devoutness and purity; she made the sign of the cross whenever a profane word escaped someone's lips.

It was a strange situation. Most of my time was spent in service to Queen Claude. But after the queen had retired to her bedchamber, I listened to the other maids of honor and *dames d'honneurs* as they bragged of the gentlemen who had paid court to them. I had little to say because I was so much younger than the others and no gentleman had yet paid me court. But I took in every word; I learned exactly what it took to charm a man and how to flatter, please, and entertain him.

And I watched as Marie sat before her silvery mirror while a serving maid fastened up her hair with jeweled combs. As soon as Marie had gone out and I was alone, I took her place before that mirror and imitated her half smile, her coy manner of turning her head slightly to one side and glancing up through her lashes, even her way of tossing her pretty curls and using her hands to call attention to her graceful neck. I practiced and practiced. I understood that I would have to learn these little gestures if I were to gain favor in my father's eyes and, when I was older, with gentlemen of the court.

My training, if that is what it was, lasted for several years. Then, when Marie was fifteen, she returned to England, where my father had secured her a place in the court of Queen Catherine. I stayed on in Paris. At first I missed my sister and her often painful little gibes, but then I ceased to think about her. Princess Renée, the king's cousin who was close to my age, became my friend and confidante.

Three years passed before I saw Marie again, at the Field of Cloth of Gold during King Henry's visit to France. At the age of thirteen I was outwardly still thin, dark, and plain. Inwardly, though, I was changing. I was growing into an alluring woman, worldly-wise and witty. I had not much longer to wait until my body was also that of a woman.

## CHAPTER 3

# Jamie Butler

## *1521–1522*

Paris glittered under a blanket of snow as the court prepared to celebrate *la Fête de Noël*—the Feast of Christmas—and I received a visit from my father, who had journeyed to France on official business from the court of Henry VIII. As we warmed ourselves by the fire in one of the royal apartments, I noticed for the first time the streaks of silver that age had woven through my father's dark beard.

"I have asked their French majesties to grant you leave to return to England with me," he said, sipping a glass of cordial.

I was stunned. I was happy where I was and had no wish to leave France. "It is as you command," I said submissively, feeling sick at heart at the thought of returning to my family. "But for what reason must I return?"

"I have arranged a betrothal for you."

A betrothal! I had not expected this, at least not for some time. I was now fourteen, but I'd hoped that betrothal was still years away. I was quite enjoying myself in the French court. I had learned to hold my own with the ladies' ribald banter in their private chambers, and I found it amusing to flirt with the gentlemen of the court. I was not interested in marriage.

Yet I found myself curious. "To whom am I to be betrothed, dear Father?" I asked.

"James Butler," he replied. "The king greatly favors the match, as does Cardinal Wolsey. James is a member of the cardinal's household."

And so, in obedience to my father's wishes, I packed up my French gowns and, soon after the beginning of the new year, bade farewell to Queen Claude, who squeezed my hand and said she was sorry to see me go; I murmured similar sentiments, as she had always been kind to me. Then I said my adieus to François, who begged to be remembered to my sister. My most heartfelt parting was from Princess Renée. We both wept many tears and exchanged tokens and promises to write.

My governess, Lady Guildford, was happy to leave France, but scarcely had we set sail from Calais than the poor lady again succumbed to seasickness, weeping and moaning. In due course we stepped ashore at Dover. I had been away from England and from my family for eight years and felt that all were strangers to me.

Members of my father's household were on hand to accompany us to Hever, and I noticed at once that these servants were not so handsomely liveried as those in Paris. My childhood home was not at all as I remembered it; Hever seemed smaller and less grand, a poor place compared to the great palaces of the Continent. My mother's once-beautiful face had aged, but she welcomed me with happy tears, remarking over and over upon what a fine lady I had become. My brother had grown tall and seemed determined to mimic my father's habit of shouting when his wishes were not instantly obeyed. My sister and her new husband, Will Carey, were at court.

"There is nothing of interest here to distract me," I wrote in the first of many complaining letters to my friend, Princess Renée. "No banquets or dancing, no witty conversation. I think I shall perish of boredom. And thus far not a word has been spoken of my betrothal to James Butler, whoever he may be."

But then my father brought word that he had secured for me a position at Queen Catherine's court. Thenceforth, my home would be with the queen, and since King Henry was fondest of his great palace at Greenwich, that is where Queen Catherine would likely spend much of her time. The news that I was going to court, even one as dull as I believed Queen Catherine's likely to be, cheered me. I wrote again to Renée, excitedly this time: "I shall often be in the presence of our magnificent king!"

Lady Alice Willoughby, the mother of the maids, took me in hand once I arrived at Greenwich. With a scowl that seemed permanently etched on her broad face, she stood with her arms folded over her ample bosom and looked me up and down. I felt myself growing smaller under her critical gaze.

Lady Alice beckoned me to follow her and led me to a chamber in the queen's apartments. The maids of honor, who were chattering among themselves when I entered, suddenly fell silent, staring at me. "Lady Anne Boleyn," announced Lady Alice loudly. "She is to share Lady Honor's bed. Be so kind as to instruct her in her duties." With that, the matron gathered up her wide skirts and disappeared.

"You are the sister of Lady Mary Boleyn? Now Lady Mary Carey?" asked the boldest of the lot, who turned out to be Lady Honor Finch, my bedmate.

"I am," I said, and I thought I heard suppressed giggles.

"You look nothing like her," ventured another.

"Why should I?" I responded.

The maids—I counted eleven of them—watched out of the corners of their pale blue eyes as I unpacked my trunks and hung my elegant French gowns on the wooden pegs assigned to me. I heard them whispering among themselves: "...dark," one murmured; "...not at all beautiful like her sister."

Lady Honor continued to ask peevish questions: "Lady Anne, why do you wear that jewel on a ribbon about your neck?"

"It is a French custom," I lied. "The king of France chooses certain of his favorites and gives them each a jewel. Ever after, they wear the jewel as a badge of the king's affection."

Lady Honor stared at me, quite dumbstruck. Then she screwed up her face and asked in a mocking tone, "Then why does your sister, Lady Mary, not wear such a jewel? She has told us that she was a *great* favorite of King Francis."

I could not mistake her meaning. "Would that not be insulting to our own king?" I demanded haughtily. "For I understand that she is now a *great* favorite of King Henry."

"So Lady Mary has let everyone know," said Lady Honor, her pale little eyes widening. "The queen detests your sister for this. I would take care, if I were you," she added, "for Her Majesty is bound to detest you as well."

"I need no such warning," I replied tartly. "The queen will find no reason to turn against me." I spoke with far more confidence than I actually felt, but I was determined that I would not pay the cost of my sister's reputation.

Thus I held my own during those first difficult days, but at night, as I lay beside Lady Honor in the narrow bed, I shed many silent tears and longed to be back in France.

THE FIRST IMPORTANT event after my arrival at the court of Henry VIII was the celebration of Candlemas on the second of February, honoring the purification of the Virgin Mary. With the queen and her retinue, I attended Mass celebrated by Cardinal Wolsey. He was a rotund figure robed in crimson, with cold eyes and a chilling smile. I disliked him on sight.

Oh, but King Henry was all anyone could wish for! At the feast that followed the blessing of the candles, I could scarcely take my eyes from him. He seemed at the age of thirty-one almost godlike, the tallest man in the court, the most vigorous and forceful of manner, and the most splendid in his person. Dressed in opulent robes studded with jewels and seated beneath his richly embroidered cloth of estate, King Henry made every man around him seem insignificant by comparison.

Next to him sat his wife, Queen Catherine. A much older woman whose looks had long since faded, she presented an unfortunate contrast to her husband. Also present was the king's six-year-old daughter, Princess Mary, a delicate child with her father's red-gold hair and blue eyes. The king doted on the little princess, parading her around the Great Hall for all to see and admire.

"When the festivities are ended," Lady Honor Finch advised me that night, "Princess Mary will be returned to her manor house in the country with her governess. But we are sure to see more of her. She is soon to be betrothed."

"To whom?" I asked Lady Honor as we each struggled for a greater share of the shrunken wool coverlet.

"The queen's nephew, Emperor Charles. The emperor's ambassadors are expected to arrive within the month to conclude the negotiations for the betrothal. It will be exciting. I love betrothal ceremonies."

"Emperor Charles? I was with him at the court of his regent, Margaret of Austria. I know him well," I said, exaggerating greatly. In truth, he had paid me no attention. Charles was a moody boy of fourteen then, waiting restlessly to reach the age at which he would rule the Netherlands in his own right.

But Honor was not impressed. She turned on her side and was soon fast asleep. I lay awake, unable to clear my mind of the vision of the magnificent King Henry and wondering how I might attract his notice.

Over the coming weeks I tried to learn what was expected of me in the queen's court. Most of the maids continued to ignore me. Even my own sister, who, as a married woman, was now a lady-in-waiting and outranked me, generally pretended to be unaware of my existence. Lady Honor and her cousin, Lady Constance—both of them as soft and bland as puddings—criticized my French gowns, my French manners, even the way I wore my hair.

Oddly, it was only my servant, Nell, a plain girl with freckled skin and one eye that turned inward, who seemed to offer friendship in addition to performing her duties well.

"The other ladies are jealous of you," Nell informed me as she combed my long, dark hair.

"But of what can they be jealous?"

"Because you are so different from the rest of them," she said, "and you are bound to attract attention. Also, you are Lady Mary's sister. They are all jealous of her as well, because she has the king's favor, and they would, every one of them, trade places with her in a trice."

*As would I,* I thought, but said nothing.

TOWARD THE END of February, the queen's court left Greenwich and traveled by barge up the River Thames to London. This was my first visit to the great capital, and naturally I was excited. Nell, the daughter of a blacksmith, had grown up in the city, and so I bade her join me and point out the sights as I stood on the windswept deck, bundled in my heavy cloak.

"That is the Tower of London," she explained as

we glided past a great fortress of towers surrounded by stone walls, "and there is Traitors' Gate. Condemned prisoners enter there, poor souls, to await beheading on Tower Hill, just beyond." I shivered and urged her to speak of other matters.

When we reached York Place, the home of Cardinal Wolsey, we were shown to the chambers where we were to be lodged. I was much impressed by the rich furnishings, the tapestries and paintings, more splendid than anything I had seen in Mechelen or Paris and certainly more opulent than those at Greenwich.

Soon my sister, Mary, who had traveled on the queen's barge, sought me out with the news: Eight of the queen's ladies had been chosen to take part in a masque for the entertainment of the emperor's ambassadors. "You are to be among them," Mary said, "for this will be your debut at court. Do try to make a good impression." I bit my tongue and said nothing about the impression that *she* had obviously made.

Besides my sister, the other dancers included the king's sister, formerly Queen Mary of France but now the wife of Charles Brandon. "The king has forgiven them," my sister whispered, "but only after they paid over enormous sums of money to Cardinal Wolsey to ease their way back into the king's good graces."

*Such power Wolsey has,* I thought, *even over the king's own sister!*

The cardinal had ordered construction at one end

of the Great Hall of an elaborate make-believe castle, complete with battlements and towers. The ladies were cast as the Virtues of the Perfect Mistress: the king's sister would play Beauty, I was to play Perseverance, and my sister would portray Kindness, which I thought laughably inaccurate.

We Virtues were to be gowned in white satin trimmed in yellow, our bonnets draped with gold veils. In addition to the dancers, several choristers would represent the Feminine Vices, such as Danger, Disdain, and Sharp Tongue. I frankly thought the Vices more interesting than the Virtues.

These English ladies seemed to me a graceless lot; they had none of the French manner in which I had been trained. We endured a number of rehearsals, involving everyone but the king, who would portray one of the Masculine Virtues. The king was known to be a splendid dancer, but even if he'd had two left feet, no one would have dared suggest that he needed improvement. My sister's dashing husband, Will Carey, was also one of the Masculine Virtues, and, I learned, so was James Butler.

Will had been assigned the task of presenting my soon-to-be-betrothed to me. He also explained why my father was pursuing this betrothal: "The marriage will solve an inheritance problem."

James was the son of Piers Butler, a fierce Irish warlord called "the Red," who did not give a second thought to the murder of any rival blocking his path. My grandfather, earl of Ormonde, had died several years previous, leaving a number of great estates to my mother. Piers the Red argued that he was the rightful heir and called himself earl of Ormonde, a title coveted by my father. Since no agreement was likely to be reached, it was proposed that marrying the daughter of the English faction (me) to the son of the Irish faction (James) would resolve the dispute.

"Jamie is a kind of hostage," Will explained, "kept in England by Wolsey and the king as a way of holding Piers Butler at bay. You can settle it all by marrying him."

I found Jamie comely enough, in an Irish sort of way, with a crooked smile, teeth that overlapped in the front, and glowing hazel eyes. I saw that he found me attractive, but also that he intended to master me. "You could stand with a bit of taming," he remarked, when I suggested some improvement to his missteps.

"Oh?" I replied, tilting my head to one side and looking up at him with a half smile, as French women do. "And why is that? Do you spy a bit of wildness then?"

Jamie Butler frowned. "We are to be betrothed, you know," he said. "I would not have a wife who will not obey me."

In our first conversation he had brought up the issue of obedience! "Then perhaps you would not have me as wife at all," I said sharply, and turned to walk away.

But Jamie seized me roughly, pinned my arms at my sides, and kissed me.

I did not mind being kissed, but I very much minded being seized. Furious, I struggled free of his grasp and wiped my mouth with the back of my hand to show my contempt.

Jamie glared at me. "Hellcat," he growled, and stormed off.

I determined at that moment that, although I might be forced to become betrothed to him, I would never marry Jamie Butler.

AT THE SAME TIME, I made the acquaintance of another participant in the masque, Hal Percy. Hal was a well-favored young man whose thick brown curls and lively blue eyes were set off by his costume: cap and coat of cloth of gold with blue velvet buskins and a blue satin cloak. Like Jamie, Lord Percy was a member of Cardinal Wolsey's household, which I soon found to be an unenviable position. Hal's response to my lingering looks and winsome smiles was immediate and hearty. He liked me, and I liked him far better than I did the rude Jamie Butler.

All went as planned on the day of the masque. At the crucial moment, heralded by the booming of cannons, King Henry made a dramatic entrance and led the attack upon the castle. We ladies in the tower pelted our attackers with sweetmeats and rose water, until at last the heated ardor of the gentlemen melted the cool shyness of the ladies. Conquered by love, we descended from the tower and danced with our gentlemen conquerors.

The masque was followed by a feast, where puny little Princess Mary became the center of attention. She seemed quite smug about the court paid her, especially by the foreign ambassadors. Plainly, the person whom she most adored was her father and the person whom she most feared was Cardinal Wolsey.

After the feasting, there was more dancing. My sister was often the king's partner, earning her the poisonous looks of Queen Catherine. In vain I sought to catch the king's eye, and my failure to do so was a sore disappointment to me.

In the days that followed, our dowdy queen missed no opportunity to speak to me harshly in her heavy Spanish accent. I could think of no reason for her hurtful words, for I had done nothing. Close to tears, I said as much to Lady Honor, who offered this explanation: "If Queen Catherine is rude to Lady Mary Carey, the king will hear about it from Lady Mary herself, and the queen might then suffer the king's displeasure as a result. But the queen can treat *you* as spitefully as she wishes, for there is nothing you can do about it."

WITH THE BEGINNING of Lent on Ash Wednesday, the banqueting season came to an end. For six weeks there were no more jousts, no more masques, no more dancing and extravagant feasting. I was expected to attend Mass several times daily in the company of Queen Catherine.

Then, at Easter, the court came to life again.

Everyone turned out in their finest gowns and furs and jewels for the brilliant service on Easter Eve, with Mass celebrated by Cardinal Wolsey. The banquets that followed were lively affairs, although in my opinion far less refined than in France. King Henry made several grand entrances, each time attired in a different outfit of magnificent brocade robes, shimmering satin doublets, rich velvet trunk hose, and sparkling jewels.

I wished daily for some sign of recognition from the king and received none. Too often I found myself in the company of the preening Jamie Butler, despite my efforts to avoid him. Whenever the chance arose, I put myself in the company of Hal Percy, who rewarded me with ingratiating smiles. But it was a smile from the king that I longed for.

AT THE END OF MAY, the king and queen and the little princess left Greenwich in a great procession bound for Dover to greet Charles, who was now not only king of the Netherlands but Holy Roman emperor as well. Only the queen's favorites accompanied her on the journey, while the rest of us remained behind under the supervision of Lady Alice. In truth, I welcomed the respite from my duties. During the queen's absence, I found it fairly easy to get out from under Lady Alice's nose for long periods of time—time that I spent engaging the attentions of Hal Percy, whom I found more and more appealing.

When messengers heralded the arrival of the procession returning from Dover, we all gathered to welcome not only our own people but also the emperor's enormous retinue. No longer the awkward boy I remembered from our days at Mechelen, Charles was a man of twenty-two with a large chin and a pleasant manner. His austere black velvet clothing contrasted dramatically with the ornate silks and colorful velvets of the English nobility.

Once her betrothal ceremony was over, Princess Mary was returned to her country manor in Hatfield, and Emperor Charles took up residence at Bridewell, a beautiful palace renovated by King Henry for the imperial visit. In July, the king and queen left on summer progress, riding into the countryside with their great retinue for their annual round of visits and lodging for extended periods in the homes of various members of the nobility.

I was not included in the royal entourage, nor was my sister. Instead, I was sent to stay with Mary while her husband, Will, accompanied the royal couple. Both of us were disappointed at being left behind, and I suspect that we were both thinking of King Henry, for each of us contrived to make him the frequent subject of our conversation.

"The king has written a song for me," Mary informed me, more than a little smugly. "Shall I sing it?" Without waiting for my reply, she treated me to a few lines:

*As the holly groweth green*
*and never changeth hue,*
*So I am—ever have been—*
*unto my lady true.*

"And you are that lady?" I asked skeptically.

"I am sure of it," said Mary.

Later, as we strolled one evening in her rose garden, Mary spoke of my betrothal to Jamie Butler. "Has there been further word from Father?" she asked.

"None," I said. "Nor have I inquired about it, for I sincerely hope that it will not come to pass."

"But why not? You could do worse—assuming you can stay at a safe distance from old Piers the Red."

"The father at least sounds interesting," I told her. "I find the son irresolute, fainthearted, and pusillanimous. His boldest move was his ridiculous attempt to kiss me."

Mary laughed. "I would consider that act neither irresolute nor fainthearted," she said. "As for pusillanimous, I know not the meaning of the word."

CHAPTER 4

# Lord Hal

## *1522–1523*

The warm and often damp weeks of summer gave way to cool, crisp autumn, and the royal court once again gathered at Greenwich. I welcomed the change of scene and was glad to be away from the constant presence of my sister, who often angered me with her little taunts, some unwitting, most not. My family was much involved in court activities, but I saw little of them except George, who hung about, gambling at dice with the servants when he should have been with his tutors.

At the end of November, we entered the season of Advent and counted off the days of preparation for the Feast of the Nativity. I did as the queen required of me and hoped that she would not pay me much notice; I had no desire to be a scapegoat for my sister. And I dared not question my father about Jamie Butler.

"Sweet sister Renée," I wrote to my dear friend in Paris, "My father merely informs me that Cardinal Wolsey will see to my betrothal, but that the negotiations will take time, as both parties move forward with great deliberation. But I wonder—what if Jamie Butler insists that we leave England and make our home in Ireland? I have heard that the Irish are wild barbarians with only the merest pretense of refinement. The idea of living among them fills me with dread."

Even when I was at court, my life at times seemed very dull, and I yearned for something exciting to happen. I often wished myself back in France, where gaiety reigned no matter what the season. To amuse myself I flirted with Hal Percy and gazed at King Henry whenever the chance presented itself. I suffered occasional bouts of jealousy of my sister, which became almost unbearable when she bragged that King Henry had named one of his ships for her.

"The *Mary Boleyn* carries a crew of seventy-nine," Mary boasted. "A lovely ship, indeed."

No wonder the queen detested my sister and frequently took out her displeasure upon me!

On the Eve of Christmas, as Nell helped me into my petticoat and gown, I wondered aloud if the celebration could possibly be as amusing in England as it was in France. "No matter," said Nell. "The king will be present. No doubt Your Ladyship will find pleasure enough in that." I glanced at her quickly, but her serene face never revealed her thoughts.

I was fifteen now and no longer the youngest lady at court. And I had finally begun to attract attention. I looked nothing like the fair-skinned English ladies in their overwrought gowns, and I decided to make the most of my singularity. Rather than confining my abundant black hair in a headdress, as the others usually did, I wore it loose upon my shoulders. I was still rather thin, my bosom would never be as generous as my sister's, but the gowns I'd brought from Paris showed off my womanliness to good advantage. Having caught their eye, I trifled with the gentlemen of the court, playing at the game of love according to the rules I'd learned in France. I longed to test my charms on King Henry, but he continued to devote most of his attentions to my sister and, I heard, engaged in minor dalliances with lesser ladies of Catherine's court.

And I found my fondness growing for Hal Percy, who had proved no test at all.

At the first Yuletide banquet, Lord Percy had one of his servants deliver to me a confit wrapped in a bit of paper on which he had scribbled a few lines of verse. The poetry was indifferent, but when I saw Hal's eyes upon me, I smiled and touched my fingers to my lips as a kiss.

Night after night of Yuletide we of the court supped and danced until we were too weary to continue. I had the pleasure of many partners for the galliards and the pavanes. Each time Lord Percy invited me to dance, I accepted him—his dancing was more proficient than his poetry—but I confess that all the while I was keeping my eye on King Henry.

Twelfth Night was a time of misbehavior and mischief, far more boisterous than anything I had experienced in Paris. One would never have ridden a horse into the Great Hall of the French king's palace in the midst of a banquet, as did the Lord of Misrule at King Henry's celebration!

After hours of feasting and carousing, my head pounded from the drunken shouting and my eyes stung with smoke from the fire and the smoldering torches. Allowing those around me to think I was hurrying to the garderobe to relieve myself, I rushed out of the noisy, smoky hall and into the courtyard. Snow had fallen, but now a quarter moon and a scattering of stars shone brilliantly in the cloudless night sky. Breathing deeply, I drew my cloak close about me and hurried toward the gate, leaving a trail of dark footprints in the wet snow.

Someone called my name: "Anne! Lady Anne!"

I looked over my shoulder. Lord Percy was pursuing me. I scooped up a handful of snow and flung it at him. Then I turned and started to run. But I could not run fast enough through the snow to escape him. Nor did I want to. The roars of laughter in the Great Hall could still be heard when Hal caught up to me. I hurled more snow; he threw some back at me, both of us laughing breathlessly. Abruptly the game ended, and Hal wrapped me tight in his arms and kissed me. I responded with lips as eager as his.

Our kiss went on and on, until I realized that I must stop it. I pushed him away, but without the contempt that I'd shown Jamie Butler. "This cannot be," I told him. "Have you not considered that perhaps I may be betrothed?"

Hal simply laughed. "What care I?" he said boldly, and tried to sweep me into his embrace once more.

But I eluded him. "Sir!" I cried, and hurried away, plunging back into the turmoil of the Great Hall, where no one even noticed that I had been away longer than should have been necessary and that my boots and my petticoats were wet with snow.

I ASSUMED THAT Hal Percy had imbibed too much spiced wine at the raucous Twelfth Night festivities and thus had found the courage to kiss me. I thought it an evening's trifle. Hal Percy did not dismiss it so lightly.

The maids in the queen's chambers were well acquainted with Lord Percy and spoke eagerly of him, for he was both pleasing and highborn, the son of the wealthy and powerful earl of Northumberland. Now he became a frequent visitor to the queen's apartments, where he much amused the ladies with his cleverness. I looked forward eagerly to his witty conversation and his pretty songs, which I knew were intended for my pleasure. Increasingly, I found myself drawn to him, and I thought he might be falling in love with me. As the weeks passed, I realized that I was falling in love with him as well.

At a certain signal—I would touch the jewel at my throat—he would make his farewells to the ladies and leave us. Shortly thereafter I would find an excuse to go out. I knew of many secluded cabinets and darkened alcoves around the palace where we could meet in secret.

This was my first taste of love. The risk of discovery increased our excitement as we exchanged sweet words and sweeter kisses. After a time, I would tear myself away and hurry back to my needlework or whatever bit of nonsense I was supposedly attending to. There were so many of us that one maid of honor was scarcely missed—certainly not by Lady Alice, mother of the maids, who in her dotage seemed unable to count past twelve. Much harder to deceive was Lady Honor, who, it seemed, had also fallen in love. At first I had no notion what ailed her as she sighed and moped about. Then I pressed her to confess.

"Oh, I know that it is hopeless," she sniveled. "I yearn for just a smile, a private word with him, but I am sure the gentleman of whom I speak loves someone else!"

"Of whom *do* you speak, Lady Honor?" I asked, in all innocence, for I truly had no idea.

"Why, of Lord Percy!" she exclaimed, amazed

that I hadn't guessed at once. "Have you not noticed how he lingers about the queen's apartments?"

"Yes, I have noticed," I said, covering my surprise and pretending to ponder her question. "But I cannot guess which lady's favors he seeks."

"Nor can I," sighed Lady Honor. "Although I believe Lady Constance loves him as well."

Poor Honor! I managed not to smile. "So you have set your cap at him then?" I asked.

Two tears coursed down her wan cheeks. "No, I have not, for it is of no use—for the other lady as well as for me! Lord Percy is betrothed to Mary Talbot, daughter of the earl of Shrewsbury. They have been pledged since they were children."

I felt the blood drain from my face, and my mouth went dry as chalk. It took a great effort to conceal from Lady Honor my feelings of shock and betrayal. In all our secret trysts, Hal had uttered not one single word about a betrothal! But, I confess, neither had I spoken forthrightly to him of Jamie Butler, although I had hinted at a pending arrangement. No wonder Hal had shown no concern! Since I'd heard nothing for months about negotiations for the Butler betrothal, I had allowed myself to hope that it might never happen. But, if Honor was to be believed, Hal's betrothal was real and binding. I felt deeply wounded and angry at him for treating me so carelessly, and I resolved to challenge him with what I had learned. In a week's time Lord Percy would return to York Place with Wolsey for Lent, forty days of tedious fasting and prayer. We would see no more of each other until Passiontide, and I did not wish to wait that long to have it out with him.

At Shrovetide, the three days before Ash Wednesday, King Henry arranged a joust and several banquets. I had been sleeping little and eating hardly at all—a condition that did not escape the notice of my bedmate, Lady Honor. I determined to speak to Hal that night about the matter over which I had been brooding.

"What ails you, Lady Anne?" asked Honor that afternoon, feigning concern. "You seem unwell. Should we ask Lady Alice for a purgative?"

I brushed her aside. The cure I needed was a goodly hour alone with Hal, but although he was often within my sight, there were always people about.

Hal attended the final Shrovetide banquet, as did everyone else, including my parents, my brother, and my sister. Caught up with my determination to take this last opportunity to question Hal, I paid no particular attention to the looks that passed between my sister and the king. But I did take notice when Lady Mary Carey dropped her handkerchief, in plain view of the king (and the queen!). One of the king's courtiers retrieved it for her. Soon the king departed by one door, my sister by another.

Not long after, Hal glanced my way, and I touched the jewel at my throat. Moments later we managed to slip into the wardrobe where properties and costumes for the masques were kept, a secret place we had visited several times before. Hal moved immediately to embrace me, but I pushed him away angrily, determined to speak my piece. Before I could utter a word, however, we heard a deep male voice close by, followed by muffled peals of feminine laughter. We both recognized that voice—King Henry. The laugh, of course, was my sister's.

There was no way that we could leave the wardrobe without calling attention to ourselves. And so we stayed where we were, hidden among the folds of the costumes, listening to Mary and the king, my heart pounding with fear of discovery. By the time the king and my sister had gone out by separate doors, we could afford to be absent no longer. I'd had no opportunity to challenge Lord Percy concerning the matter of his betrothal to Mary Talbot. Now I would have to wait until Easter. I refused Hal's parting kiss, then dragged myself back to my place in the Great Hall, doing my best to disguise my misery.

While we were apart through the dreary weeks of Lent, Hal wrote me long passionate letters, pleading to know why I had been so cold to him during our last encounter. I begged him stop, lest someone discover one of the letters—Lady Honor, for instance. As the days passed, I found that I missed him. Perhaps Honor was wrong, I thought, and no betrothal existed. Perhaps there was a simple explanation, and all would be well. The long separation slowly melted my anger.

At last, Lent ended, and the court cast off its gloomy pall at the Great Feast of Easter. When I saw Hal Percy again after our six weeks apart, I welcomed his embrace. Surely Honor was wrong. I shut my eyes to the possible truth, and we began to meet more and more often, employing less and less caution. I enjoyed the recklessness of our secret meetings. Nell became adept at standing watch, warning us of intruders with a birdlike whistle.

But there was still the matter of Jamie Butler. "One day soon we shall become betrothed, Lady Anne," Jamie said whenever he managed to have me to himself for a moment or two by encountering me as I performed an errand for the queen or seeking me out as a dancing partner.

Jamie had adopted a fawning manner that annoyed me. He had abandoned his threats to tame me, which I saw now as empty. Unlike his warrior father, he had no will at all. Far more to my liking was the impetuous, hot-blooded behavior of dear Hal.

"I am determined to have you for my wife, darling Anne," Hal whispered one fine June day when we had slipped away.

*And why not?* I thought. The negotiations for the Butler marriage seemed to be going nowhere, for which I was grateful. Hal Percy had wealth and would one day inherit titles and even greater wealth. I had neither. My father would surely be pleased that I had made such a fine match for myself. If Lord Percy wished to marry beneath his station, that was his concern, not mine. The king's sister had done so, and she glowed with happiness. But there remained the unresolved matter of Hal's prior betrothal.

"I would gladly accept your proposal, were it not for Mary Talbot," I told him, at last daring to broach the subject and trembling as I did so.

"Dearest Anne," said Hal, "I have no wish at all to marry Lady Mary Talbot, nor, I am told, does she have any wish to marry me. The lady and I shall simply inform our parents of our desires. She may have already done so. I beg you, Anne, be my love! Be my wife! Pledge yourself to me!"

I didn't hesitate. "Yes, dear Hal," I said, as little ripples of joy surged in my breast, "I shall pledge myself to you with all my heart."

Two weeks later, on my sixteenth birthday, a lovely, bright summer day, Nell helped me to dress in a new gown of pale green silk and wove flowers in my hair. She put on the kirtle and pretty cap I'd given her, and together we slipped away from the manor house where the queen's court was lodged and hurried to meet Lord Percy.

We waited in a copse of yews at the edge of a meadow. As the sun made its steady arc across the cloudless sky, Nell and I passed the time by decking a small bower with primroses and ivy. *Has he changed his mind?* I worried as an hour went by, then two. *Has he been discovered?* I became increasingly uneasy that our plans had gone awry. Nell did her best to calm me.

At last Hal arrived, entirely disheveled, humbly begging my pardon—he had been ordered to accompany the king on a hunt. Even with his hose muddied and his cap askew, Hal Percy sparked a flame in me. I sent Nell to stand watch, and together Hal and I knelt in the bower. Without a priest or any witness save God above, we joined hands and pledged ourselves to each other, sealing our pledge with a passionate kiss.

Thereafter, foolishly believing there was no further need for secrecy, we were entirely open about being sweethearts. I looked forward to a fine future as Hal's wife. At last I was happy.

Happy, that is, except when forced to look upon the sour countenance of Lady Honor. "My heart is broken into a thousand pieces," she wailed, "and you are the cause of it!"

"Surely, Lady Honor, he is not the only fish in the sea!" I reminded her. But it did no good. She continued to mope and glare.

I could ignore Lady Honor's pouts and the disapproving looks of the other maids as Hal and I twittered together shamelessly. But gossip spread quickly. When word of what we had done reached the ears of Cardinal Wolsey, the cardinal erupted in fury. I had to listen to a description of all that happened from Lady Honor herself. Her brother, John Finch, was a member of the chancellor's household and had witnessed Wolsey's rage. Honor made no effort to conceal her satisfaction as she told me what she'd heard.

Wolsey, a close friend of Hal's father, the earl of Northumberland, knew of the Percys' prior contract with the Talbots. Wolsey immediately wrote to the earl, describing Hal's folly. Wolsey also informed King Henry, who, according to John Finch, ordered his chancellor to separate Lord Percy from Thomas Boleyn's daughter. Wolsey summoned Hal and lectured him on his responsibilities as heir to the earldom, reminding Hal that he had no business speaking of marriage to any lady without the permission of his father and his king. And—most outrageously—Wolsey told Hal that, had he let his wishes be known, the king would have found him a suitable, nobly born lady to marry.

"And then," Honor said, gleefully repeating her brother's words, "the chancellor told Lord Percy that he must submit to his father's will or be disinherited."

I was shocked by this turn of events, but I drew myself up proudly to conceal my pain. "I am certain that Lord Percy spoke well in my defense," I said, although I had no idea if Hal had such courage.

"Well, yes, he did," Honor admitted reluctantly. "He defended you and your family. And then Lord Percy wept—he actually wept!—saying that the two of you had made an agreement to marry, and he could not break this binding pledge. He even asked Cardinal Wolsey to intercede with the king on his behalf!"

"He did?" I stammered.

"Yes, but to no avail. Wolsey told him that he

must obey the king's wishes, and that is the end of it." Lady Honor, obviously relishing her duty, next informed me that Wolsey had summoned the earl of Northumberland to speak to Hal.

"Lord Percy's father was furious at his son for bringing down the wrath of the king upon the Percy family," Honor reported. "He flung many harsh words at Lord Percy, calling him proud, presumptuous, and disdainful, and insisting that the pledges he made to you be nullified. To win his father's forgiveness, and the king's, Lord Percy yielded at last and promised never to see you again."

Oh, how I hated the triumph in her voice as Honor delivered that piece of news! Haughtily I lifted my chin and swept away without a word, determined not to let her see my distress.

All my hopes had been dashed. I wept many bitter tears, witnessed only by Nell. The two pudding cousins—Honor and Constance—treated me with honeyed kindness, but I was certain they gloated over my misery. That was indeed the end of my betrothal to Hal Percy. I never again had a moment alone or a private word with Hal, and within months I learned that he was married to Mary Talbot.

If only that had ended the matter for me! Alas, it did not. Soon my father learned of my misdeed. He was furious, roaring at me of his displeasure, punctuating his odious words with slaps and kicks.

*"Brazen . . . impudent . . . hussy!"* he shouted, striking me a stinging blow across my face with each

word. "Have you no notion of what you have done? The king has ordered you banished from court! What chance have you now of contracting a good marriage? Your reputation is ruined, and there you stand, willful and proud as a queen!"

*Banished from court!* Of all the blows my father struck, that one caused the most pain. Why had the king ordered such harsh measures against me? I cried out then, but my cries bought me no mercy.

"Wolsey is correct—you are lacking in wit and common sense, as well as in virtue," my father stormed, seizing me by the shoulders and shaking me so fiercely that my sleeve tore. "There is no help for you!" With a final blow that sent me reeling, he spun on his heel and stalked out of the chamber.

I leaned against the wall, tenderly feeling for bruises, of which there were plenty. So I was banished from court. What would that mean? Back to Hever, I supposed. And then what? Had I truly ruined my life? I refused to believe that. But whatever happened to me, it was the fault of that accursed Cardinal Wolsey! The king might never have known of the affair, never have ordered my banishment, had it not been for Wolsey.

I dragged myself to my feet. My ankle had begun to swell. Painfully I limped to the maids' chambers, intending to find a basin of water and some soft linen strips to bind up the worst of my injuries.

And there sat Lady Honor, her eyes round with

wonder at my state of disarray. She opened her mouth to speak.

"Not one word, not to me or anyone else!" I hissed before she could utter a sound. She scuttled away in a fright, and I laid my head upon my arms and wept for all that was lost.

When I was drained of tears, my heart filled with bitterness. *Someday I shall have my revenge,* I vowed. *Someday Cardinal Wolsey will pay a grievous price for my humiliation.*

CHAPTER 5

# The Poet

## 1523–1525

Within days I was back at Hever, by orders of Cardinal Wolsey, who could not—or would not—say how long my banishment was to last. This put me in the worst possible temper. Here I was with nothing to do but curse my fate. Never had I been in such a wretched state. Day after day, I wept. My heart ached for Hal Percy, sentenced to a loveless union with Mary Talbot. I was grieved that King Henry, whose respect and approval I so fervently sought, now held me in great disfavor. And I nurtured a growing and implacable hatred against the cause of my plight, that fat prelate in the crimson robes, Cardinal Wolsey.

I was to be under my father's supervision at

Hever, but he was accompanying the king and queen on summer progress, and thus I did not have to endure his recriminations. My sister and her husband were also on the royal progress—the final straw! I had not even Nell to distract me, for she had been kept at Greenwich to help with the summer cleansing of the palace. My mother elected (or was ordered by my father) to stay with me. Her unshakable complacency put me into an even darker mood, which she chose to ignore, going on about her life as though nothing were amiss.

I fretted as the summer crept by. Then my father returned from progress in a lighter mood. He had received word from the king that he was to be knighted and then granted the noble title of baron, giving him even greater responsibility in the king's household. I was not invited to the ceremony. My parents were also rewarded with quarters in the palace. I sulked as they packed up their beds, tables, stools and benches, a fine cupboard, and other household goods to move to Greenwich.

Perhaps because my banishment was an embarrassment to my parents, Wolsey permitted me to return to court with them at the start of the Yuletide season. But first I had to bear more of my father's harangues.

"Do not bring further disgrace upon this family, daughter!" he growled. "God knows if we shall ever be able to find you a husband as a result of your shameful behavior."

I lowered my eyes and said nothing, although I did wonder again what had become of his negotiations for my betrothal to Jamie Butler. Was I now free of that threat? Had the scandal of Hal Percy scotched the deal? I was left to reach my own conclusions and clung to the belief that for some reason the bargaining had come to nothing. If that were true, it would be a great relief.

At first I was pleased to be back at court, but I quickly learned that life among the maids of honor was no better than before. In my exile I had almost forgotten the long dull hours of attending the queen, waiting to be sent off on some meaningless errand; meals taken in the crowded Great Hall of the palace with barking dogs and filthy beggars and brazen prostitutes; the noise and confusion of the endless boasting and bickering of the maids in our drafty chambers.

What's more, it was my ill luck to be forced again to share a hard, narrow bed with Lady Honor Finch, who was no more content with the arrangement than was I.

"And will you take another lover, Lady Anne?" Honor asked spitefully.

"I shall do whatever pleases me," I retorted.

I knew that she was jealous of me; probably they all were—those dull maids of honor with their pale yellow hair and pale white skin and pale blue eyes. How I despised them! To my face, the other maids cooed and simpered, expressing their pleasure at my presence among them. How they lied! How false were those smiles! Behind my back, they still tattled about me and Hal Percy and waited for me to fall from favor once more. I knew this was true because Nell was again in my service and full of gossip. But I swore that I would not fall, not ever again.

COURT WAS AS HECTIC as ever. A man of boundless vigor, King Henry ordered banquets, organized jousts, challenged his gentlemen to tennis and usually defeated them, conquered nearly every opponent in wrestling, dazzled onlookers with his skill at archery, gambled boldly at cards and dice, called for an audience when he played his own compositions upon the virginals and sang in a fine tenor voice. The king did not like to be alone. His great vitality required that his courtiers be in his company from early morning until late at night. It seemed that he rarely slept.

Flirtations among the ladies and gentlemen of the court were commonplace. Everyone knew about my love affair with Lord Percy and its unhappy end. Despite the scandal, or perhaps because of it, I attracted many admirers: handsome (and some not-so-handsome) young (and not-so-young) courtiers who coaxed me to walk out with them and entreated me to listen to lines of poetry they had scribbled or little jokes they wished to tell.

I enjoyed the attentions of these gentlemen, most

of them wellborn, some of wealthy families, a few intelligent and even amusing. They proved a distraction, and slowly my heart began to mend. Sometimes I accepted their kisses, lingering with them in shadowy corners. The flirtations were a game, and I was a clever player. And as I reveled in my prowess, my life improved in a way I had not foreseen. When one of the maids left court to marry a Welsh nobleman, Lady Honor moved to occupy her empty bed. For a time, at least, I had a bed—and a coverlet—to myself and had no need to reply to Honor's disagreeable questions.

And so the months passed. My seventeenth birthday came and went. But while I had many admirers at court, there had been no marriage prospects since the loathsome Cardinal Wolsey had ended my betrothal to Lord Percy. The betrothal to that doltish Irishman, Jamie Butler, had come to naught, and although he still lurked about the court, I managed to avoid him. I took care to keep my heart well guarded, and on the whole I was not displeased with my life. King Henry and Queen Catherine seemed to have forgotten my earlier transgressions, but my father reminded me that he had still not forgiven me for the scandal I'd created.

"It is your own fault that you are of marriageable age and still without a suitor," he growled.

I HAD BEEN BACK at court for a full year—long enough to hear gossip of the unhappiness of Hal

Percy's marriage to Mary Talbot—when I made the acquaintance of a man of extraordinary charm and good looks: broad brow, finely shaped nose, strong jaw enhanced by a close-trimmed beard, blue eyes brimming with wit and good humor. Noted as a poet of unusual talent at the age of twenty-one, he often joined the king in the tiltyard for jousting and at the banquet that followed. When we found occasions to meet, he sometimes recited little verses that he'd jotted down. I found myself much attracted to this man, as much—this was soon clear—as he was attracted to me. His name was Tom Wyatt.

On the Great Vigil of Easter, the entire court attended Mass, celebrated by Cardinal Wolsey, for whom my hatred had not diminished one whit. Poor old Queen Catherine wore a new gown for the occasion; even so, she was a pitiable dowd. Also present was little Princess Mary. The king trotted the puny princess around the Great Hall, showing her off.

"The perfect pearl of the world!" he bellowed. "The jewel of all England!" What was not spoken of was Princess Mary's own betrothal. Her intended, Emperor Charles V, had broken it off and pledged himself instead to marry a Portuguese princess.

I was about to steal out of the banqueting hall to meet Tom Wyatt at an agreed-upon place when I became aware of King Henry's eyes lingering upon me. I had been at court for three years (save for the months of my banishment) and in the king's presence many times over. Although I'd spent hours gazing at his splendid person, this was the first I had felt his gaze come to rest upon me and no other. As I rose from my place at the lower table where the maids supped, I glanced at the king, seated on the dais beneath the cloth of estate. For a moment our eyes met, and the king smiled. I caught my breath, feeling the blood rush to my face, and I dropped into a low curtsy. When I looked up again, the king's attention had shifted away. I collected myself and hurried off to find Tom Wyatt.

"Lady Anne!" the poet called softly, stepping out from behind a tapestry. "I have a new verse for you," he said, and fell to one knee to recite it:

*She from myself now hath me in her grace:*
*She hath in hand my wit, my will, and all.*

"It is imperfect," he apologized, rising and taking my hand. "Unlike you, my lady." And then he kissed me. This was followed by another kiss, and another. But it was not of Tom Wyatt that I was thinking as our lips met; it was of King Henry.

Secrets were hard to keep. Someone was always watching, leaping to conclusions (some false, others not), and then passing the news to someone else. Thus word began to circulate that I was Tom Wyatt's mistress. Although I did entertain the notion—the hope?—that my future might lie with Tom, I soon learned from Honor Finch of a serious impediment.

"I see that you have made the acquaintance of the poet, Tom Wyatt," observed Lady Honor, her thin lips pursed.

"Only slight," I responded, and then I hurried on, "I am told that the king thinks highly of Wyatt's verses."

"More highly, *I am told,* than Wyatt thinks of his wife," Honor sniffed. "You know of Elizabeth Wyatt, surely? That they have a child, a boy not yet four years old?"

"Of course, I know all that!" I snapped impatiently, but in truth I knew nothing of it. "He loves her not," I added, a guess that turned out to be accurate. I felt betrayed, even if that hadn't been his intention.

I wasted no time yearning for what I could not have—that much I'd learned from my unhappy experience with Hal Percy. Instead, I decided, I would turn the poet's love for me into something useful; the attentions of a charming man would surely enhance my own value among other gentlemen. With this in mind, I continued to encourage Tom in his desire to please me with his pretty verses and little tokens.

I also paid closer attention than ever before to court gossip about King Henry. The king's interest darted restlessly of late, his fancy lighting on first this lady of his wife's retinue, then that one. It was rumored that my sister had remained the king's mistress even after she'd married Will Carey. Now Mary had a child, and I assumed that her affair with the king had ended. Perhaps he was in the mood for a new mistress. Or perhaps he merely wished to engage in the pastime of courtly love.

And so I decided to attempt to engage King Henry in a flirtation. As I learned at the French court, men often desired most what they could not too easily get. The trick was to tempt him into pursuit but not allow him to capture me. I wanted the king's attention. Beyond that, I had no goal but to best the king at the one game I believed I could play as well as he: the game of love. Winning the king's heart would surely prove to my father that I was no longer the ill-favored daughter.

Tom was plainly in love with me. Now I would make certain that King Henry noticed the extravagant attention his favorite was paying me. I would use the poet to lure the king.

Honor Finch could scarcely bear it. "You are without modesty or shame!" Honor seethed. "You wear your hair loose and uncovered, as though your black hair were something to be proud of! You do not resemble the rest of us. You do not even look like an English lady! Sometimes," she continued heatedly, "I think you must be a changeling abandoned by a gypsy!"

"I assure you, Lady Honor," I replied calmly to her viperish tongue, "I am the trueborn daughter of my father and my mother, as you are of yours. Unless, of course . . . ?" I let the question hang.

My duties required that I accompany the queen about her courtly routine, to Mass several times each day (Catherine was even more pious than Queen Claude, who, I learned, had died the previous year) and to the Great Hall for banquets. As I did so, I was now often aware of the king's eyes upon me. This thrilled me, but also made me wary. Many others surely observed this as well. Gossip flew unchecked, and I had to be mindful not to excite the jealousy of the queen.

Still, the attentions of Tom Wyatt remained unwavering. I was certain that the king took note of that, too. Now I had only to wait and see what would happen next.

THE MOOD IN the queen's chambers was dark. Queen Catherine had received a message from the king, by way of Cardinal Wolsey, that we were to prepare for another ceremony. In July, Henry Fitzroy, the king's bastard son by Bessie Blount, was to be honored at Bridewell Palace at a ceremony awarding him a string of titles: Duke of Richmond, Duke of Somerset, Earl of Nottingham, Lord High Admiral, Lord Lieutenant of Ireland, Lord Warden of the Marches.

Henry Fitzroy was six years old, and hardly anyone had ever seen the boy. He was kept in the shadows, far from court, although it was said that he had the best of tutors and was treated with all the deference due the king's son. Now he would have more important titles than any given by the king to Princess Mary.

One of Queen Catherine's virtues was her abiding patience, almost unimaginable in its endurance. King Henry could fume and rant all he wished, and his wife would continue to smile at him with great forbearance. King Henry could make love to as many women as he wished, and Catherine always forgave him. But this time the queen was furious: Giving his illegitimate son all those titles was a blow to her daughter's future and an insult to her, the queen.

"This is too much to bear!" Queen Catherine cried in her heavy Spanish accent, loud enough for us all to hear. "I will not have my daughter passed over for the crown by the king's bastard!" But we all knew that there was nothing the queen could do. Her wishes, like her anger, counted for nothing.

Princess Mary, brought from far-off Ludlow Castle to Bridewell, may not have understood at first the importance of the occasion, but her mother wasted no time in telling her. "You are being left behind for the bastard Fitzroy!" Queen Catherine spat out the words within the hearing of the entire retinue.

THE DAY OF THE CEREMONY was hot and dusty. In my heavy gown I suffered silently through the tedious proceedings as little Fitzroy was made first an earl and then a duke. Each step in his elevation involved a separate array of robes and another set of rituals. I was in a position to watch the expressions of anger and grief that flitted across the face of the queen.

Of most importance to my family that day, though, was the ceremony that created my father Viscount Rochford. Thomas Boleyn had finally taken his place among the nobility, higher even than a baron; closer than ever to the king, his influence approached that of the vile Wolsey.

To the banquet that followed a day of seemingly endless ceremony, I wore a splendid new gown made of black satin embroidered with pearls and lace of gold. It set me dramatically apart from the English court ladies in their usual fusty, overly ornamented gowns. My hair rippled loose around my shoulders.

I was fortunate to have a place assigned at a table where the king, splendidly garbed and seated beneath his cloth of estate, could not fail to observe me. My companions included Tom Wyatt, whose witty banter always drew from me full-throated laughter—laughter that Lady Honor criticized as vulgar. ("She not only *looks* like a crow, but she *sounds* like one," I overheard her say to her cousin, Constance. *"Caw! Caw!"*)

King Henry sat with Queen Catherine on one side of him, looking aggrieved, and the new Prince of Wales on the other, but he paid little attention to either. Time and again the king's roving glance halted and lingered upon me. *What can he be thinking?* I wondered, pretending not to notice. But I did take care to arrange myself so that the next time his glance strayed my way, my eyes met his and held them for a heartbeat. Then I modestly lowered mine.

SOON AFTER FITZROY'S ceremony, I was invited to accompany the king and queen on their summer progress. Naturally, I was delighted.

The royal progress, I learned, was an enormous undertaking. In addition to the pages, trumpeters, standard-bearers, archers, henchmen, priests, and so forth, each invited member of the court took along his family and as many servants as were needed for their comfort (Nell was to travel with me), as well as trunks containing equipage for hunting and finery for banqueting, all loaded upon wooden carts. Among the crowd were hostlers to care for the horses, cooks to provide viands for the great column of travelers, musicians to entertain us all.

It was an equally enormous proposition for the nobleman who was to be honored with a royal visit. He was expected to house and feed the entourage of several hundred people for as long as a fortnight—even longer if the king found the hunting in the private deer parks to his satisfaction and chose to tarry.

I found it all thrilling—the noisy procession of snorting horses and rattling carts and barking dogs; knights dressed in the Tudor colors of green and white; flapping pennants displaying Queen Catherine's emblem, the pomegranate, and King Henry's rose; and, of course, the jeweled garb of the king and queen. Warned of our approach by trumpet fanfares, crowds of yeomen and townspeople lined the road-way to stare and to cheer their monarchs.

After three weeks, though, I had begun to tire of the plodding gait and the wearisome sameness of the days. One morning I challenged Tom Wyatt to a fast ride across the heath.

Tom grinned. "So long as you let me lead the way, my lady."

"There is no sport in that, Tom. I mean for you to try to keep up with me."

"What you are suggesting is dangerous," Tom warned.

"Of what dangers do you speak?" I asked with a flirtatious smile.

"I know these fields and streams as you do not," Tom told me earnestly as we allowed our horses to fall back to the rear of the procession, intending to catch up later. "I was born quite near here, in Maid-stone. It is safer for me to go ahead of you."

"I shall learn them as well!" I cried, and urged my mount into a gallop. She was a piebald mare with an unfortunate will of her own, and soon we were flying across the heath. Since daybreak the skies had been lowering, and now a fine mist began to fall. I loved the feel of it against my skin, but, as the mist thickened, I could no longer see clearly. Suddenly a tall hedge loomed directly in my path. I tried to rein in the mare and turn her aside, but she had other ideas and headed straight for the hedge. I heard Tom's urgent shouts behind me, but it was too late. I clung to the mare's long neck as her hoofs lifted off the ground.

The horse landed solidly on the far side of the hedge, but I was no longer firm in my seat and continued my flight, sailing over her head. I tumbled to earth, landing abruptly in a shallow pool. There I lay in a heap, sodden and aching, until Tom appeared, white-faced with anxiety. He leaped from his horse and knelt beside me. "My lady Anne! Are you hurt?"

I felt for breaks or signs of bleeding. There were none, but my petticoats were mud-stained and rent in several places.

"My mare...," I murmured.

"She will find her way back," Tom assured me, helping me to my feet.

I allowed Tom to use his handkerchief to wipe the mud from my face, an activity that was interrupted several times by tender kisses administered to those places on my face and hands that had received some slight injury.

"It seems, dear Lady Anne, that you are always fleeing from me. The way a deer flees from the hunter."

"But you have wife and child," I reminded him. "Therefore I must always flee, and your pursuit must always be in vain."

"Perhaps not. Surely you have heard the rumors? I have separated from my wife. She has been unfaithful to me."

I had, indeed, heard them, but I pretended otherwise. Candor was not a virtue in the game of love. And he remained married.

My mare had returned, showing no sign of repentance. Patiently she waited while Tom helped me to mount, and we set off again at a measured pace. The drizzle had become a steady rain. My hair plastered to my head and shoulders and my clothing ruined, we rejoined the company. I invented a tale of how my horse had run away with me and stumbled, tossing me into the mud. Later, as Nell dried my hair and laced me into a velvet-trimmed gown, I added further details of the mishap for the benefit of Lady Alice, Lady Honor and her cousin, and the other curious maids.

The banquet that day was held in a pavilion erected by the host to accommodate the royal visitors and their court. The king seemed in fine fettle. When the last of the many dishes had been presented, tasted, and taken away, King Henry ordered servants to fetch his virginals, and for hours the king entertained us by playing and singing music of his own composition. I recognized the song my sister claimed he had written for her. Then he called for the dancing to commence.

The host's wife was King Henry's first partner. And then, to my surprise, he chose me as his second. "Lady Anne," he said as he grasped my hand, "I am told that you suffered a mishap today. I hope that you were not injured?" It was the first time I had danced with the king, the first time we had touched. His hand was warm; mine was trembling.

"Only bruises to my pride, Your Majesty," I replied as we moved easily through the rapid steps of a galliard.

Four times that night the king returned to claim me as his partner—often enough to provoke whispers among the ladies, and, I hoped, the notice of my father. The dancing continued through the hours past midnight, until host and guests were in a state of exhaustion. Of the company, only two seemed tireless: I, exhilarated by the king's attentions, and the king himself.

The next morning King Henry was up at dawn, eager to go hawking. And then an extraordinary thing happened, of which we learned later. While following his hawk, the king attempted to vault over a stream. The wooden pole broke under the king's weight, plunging him headfirst into mud so thick that he would have suffocated had it not been for the quick action of a friend. The friend was Tom Wyatt.

Naturally, the king's narrow escape was the talk of the banquet that evening, where King Henry celebrated his rescue, proposing toast after toast to the embarrassed poet.

When the dancing began and the king once again sought me as his partner, I dared to twit him, turning back on him his words to me: "I am told that Your

Majesty suffered a serious mishap today. I hope that you were not injured?"

"Only bruises to my pride, Lady Anne," King Henry replied. Then he added, quoting from Holy Scripture, "Pride goeth before destruction, and a haughty spirit before a fall."

"Then certainly I am guilty of a haughty spirit," I said, laughing.

"That haughty spirit is the source of your great charm," said the king, keeping hold of my hand far longer than the dance required.

That night I was too excited to sleep. The game of love was in play.

CHAPTER 6

# The Game of Love

## 1525–1526

With the first cool days of autumn, the royal progress came to an end, the members of the court returned to their estates, and I went to Hever with my sister, who brought her little daughter, Catherine, to visit. When we were at court or on progress, I managed to keep my distance from Mary and her sly taunts, but at Hever there was no avoiding her. Mary and I passed the afternoon hours in the gardens, where little Catherine amused herself by creeping into the bushes and then toddling back, first to her mother and then to me, blossoms crushed in her fat little fists.

As we rested in a sunny bower, sheltered from a

chill breeze, sipping goblets of hippocras, our conversation found its way to King Henry, as it inevitably did.

"The king seems somewhat downcast of late, have you noticed?" asked Mary.

"I have not. He appeared both jovial and tireless on the royal progress, hunting all day and dancing half the night."

*And surely,* I thought, *you noticed that he was dancing with* me.

"Do not be deceived by appearances. Will tells me that King Henry has much to trouble him. He has increased taxes to support his vast expenditures, and the people are resentful. The king believes himself ill-treated by Emperor Charles, who broke his betrothal to the princess. But the most important thing is this," Mary continued, bending down to accept the latest offering from her daughter. "The king badly wants—nay, *demands*—an heir to succeed him as the next ruler of England."

"What of Princess Mary?" I asked. "Or young Henry Fitzroy? We have attended ceremonies in which each received royal titles. Are they not his heirs?"

Mary Carey toyed with her ring—a ring, I remembered, that King Henry had once given her. "The king needs a legitimate male heir. The royal children each satisfy but half—Mary is legitimate but a female; Fitzroy is male but a bastard."

"Is there no chance that Queen Catherine will produce a suitable heir?" I asked, although I was certain I knew the answer.

"None whatsoever," my sister said with a dismissive wave of her hand. "The queen has had numerous pregnancies, but only one surviving child to show for it. An infant son died within weeks of its birth. Now King Henry is becoming restive. The queen is too old to bear more children, and, besides, he long ago lost interest in her. *Completely,*" my sister added, her brows arched knowingly.

"King Henry is in the mood for a new mistress," Mary continued. "He demands little of a mistress but amusement, and he gives fine gifts. You could be next, you know. Why waste your time on that poet? He is already married and has no wealth."

I was shocked by the boldness of her suggestion, but before I could utter a reply, a servant appeared to refill our goblets. I wished to hear more about the king and his mistresses, but Mary abruptly changed the subject when the servant had withdrawn.

"I have good news," she said, smiling at me over the rim of her goblet. "I am expecting another child."

"How wonderful!" I said, relieved at the new direction of our talk. "When is your confinement?"

"March," she said, turning her attention again to little Catherine. "William is quite pleased."

That explained why she appeared so willing to

yield her place as the king's favorite. *Are you carrying the king's child?* I wondered, but of course I dared not ask.

I RETURNED TO COURT at Yuletide, although the season was not so merry as one wished. London had seen many deaths from plague, and the king and queen decided to keep a quiet Christmas at Richmond Palace, upriver from the city.

By February the crisis had passed, and the king ordered a Shrovetide joust. Bundled in furs against the cold, we gathered in the tiltyards to watch the competition. King Henry cut a splendid figure, mounted on his great white stallion and clad in armor that glinted in the winter sun.

Many of King Henry's closest friends were in his company—Henry Norris; William Brereton; the king's brother-in-law, Charles Brandon—and all got the worst of it, as usual, unseated by the powerful thrusts of the king's lance. Tom Wyatt undertook to ride against the quintain, a revolving wooden figure that, if not struck accurately, swings around and strikes the unfortunate horseman a mighty blow on the back. I knew that he wanted to ride well for my sake, but poor Tom was thwacked painfully by the whirling quintain.

The king excelled at tilting. Holding his heavy wooden lance pointed straight ahead, he rode at full gallop toward a series of small metal rings. He seldom failed to hook one of the rings on each pass. With more rings jingling on his lance than any of his friends had managed to collect, King Henry rode over to the royal box where I sat watching with Queen Catherine and the ladies of the court. With a great flourish, King Henry presented the rings—not to the queen, to whom the joust had been dedicated, but to *me.* Everyone stared, none more so than the queen; a few of the ladies gasped loud enough to be heard. I, too, was frankly stunned by his open show of attention to me.

"His Majesty does me great honor," I murmured.

Queen Catherine rose unsmiling from her seat and swept out of the tiltyard. Avoiding my eyes, her ladies hurried after her. Only Lady Honor gaped openly as I passed the collection of rings to the king's usher, retaining just one as a souvenir of this event.

At the banquet I pretended not to notice that King Henry was observing me. When the dancing began, I expected the king to take me as his partner, but he did not. *Why?* I wondered. *Has his attention already turned to someone else? Then why does he watch me so closely?*

Luckily, Tom Wyatt appeared, and I devoted myself to him. That my thoughts were elsewhere must have been apparent. "My lady seems distracted," Wyatt said, but I smilingly denied that I thought of any but him.

Lent began, and several times each day for the next forty days I knelt in the chapel royal, pretending to pray but thinking only of King Henry and wondering if I occupied the king's thoughts as well. He gave me no sign. But when the banqueting and jousting and other enjoyments of court life resumed at Easter, King Henry again contrived chance encounters with me. Soon, I believed, the king would make his intentions known. My nerves were as finely tuned as the strings of my harp.

Weeks passed. Then one midsummer evening as I supped in the maids' chambers, only half listening to their ceaseless chatter, a royal page appeared. The maids fell silent as the boy delivered to me a note. Written in French, it bade me come at once; it was signed *Henricus Rex*—Henry the King—and bore the king's seal.

He wanted me *now.* I had no opportunity to change my gown, arrange my hair, or do any of those things which a lady might wish to do in preparation for such an interview, no time to become unnerved by this new course I sensed my life was about to take.

I followed the young page, not to the king's privy chamber, as I had expected, but to an even more private chamber beyond it. King Henry sprawled at his ease behind an enormous table. It appeared that he had been playing draughts, for there was the black-and-red checkered board, but no sign of an opponent. The chamber was empty, save for the king and me. Beyond the open door to a bedchamber I glimpsed an immense bed with several thick mattresses and curtains of blue velvet trimmed with gold.

I dropped to one knee, advanced, dropped a second and then a third time, reverencing the king as he required. "Your Majesty," I murmured, my eyes lowered modestly. This was the first time I had been alone with him. Slowly I raised my eyes and waited, my heart racing.

King Henry leaned toward me, his elbows on the table, his blue eyes lively, his smile winning. "Lady Anne." He breathed my name as though it were a sigh.

"Your Majesty," I said again, still kneeling. I allowed his gaze to wander over me from head to foot.

"You do please me greatly," said King Henry, and raised me up.

"It pleases me much to please you, Your Majesty," I replied.

"Good," he said. "And would it please you just as much to be the king's mistress?" he asked, stroking his close-trimmed beard.

There was no mistaking his meaning, and I had long prepared myself for just such an invitation. I well knew there were two kinds of "mistress." First was the courtly mistress, to whom romantic poems and tender looks were addressed, and with whom chaste kisses and tokens of love might be exchanged. Second was the *other* kind of mistress—a lover. I understood that King Henry spoke of the latter kind. I was to replace my sister, Mary.

I also understood that, should I yield, I would immediately lose my advantage. I knew well what became of the king's former mistresses—my sister, for one; Bessie Blount, for another: When he tired of them, as he always did, they were discarded and then married off to a willing courtier. I was certain that many ladies had been approached in this manner by the king; I doubted that any had either the desire or the will to refuse what he asked of her. Who would have dared?

I did.

I dared because I wanted so much more from King Henry. I wanted the love of his heart and his soul, which I knew would be much harder to win. Once again I was a little girl on a storm-tossed ship, bound for an uncertain future—frightened, but also exhilarated.

Now I drew a careful breath and replied with feeling, "It flatters me to believe that Your Majesty thinks so highly of me. But surely Your Majesty understands that it is no small thing that he asks. My virtue and my honor are of the greatest value to me, and I cannot risk the loss of them."

My heart was hammering loudly as I made this bold claim of virtue and honor, for I knew that my reputation had been badly damaged by my betrothal to Hal Percy. I clasped my hands to still their shaking and waited for the king's response.

King Henry stared at me in amazement. "Are you *spurning* me, Lady Anne?"

I was trembling, but my voice remained strong. "Spurn the wishes of my king? Never! Surely, I could wish for no higher honor than the undeserved attentions of the handsomest and most godly man in all Christendom! But, I must weigh the cost to my reputation. I beg you, my lord, give me time to think on it."

"Then I bid you good night, madam!" said the king brusquely. "We shall talk another time."

"Nothing would please me more, Your Majesty," I murmured, and repeated the ritual, kneeling three times as I backed out of the king's chamber. As I ran through the several passageways on my way back to the maids' apartments, I could not help smiling to myself. The score: Lady Anne, one point; King Henry, naught.

NOT LONG AFTER that interview, the king and queen prepared to leave on summer progress. I was again invited, along with my parents, to be a part of the royal retinue, and I ached to go. But before the day of their departure, I asked to be allowed to return home to Hever.

There was guile in my request. I believed that King Henry, once he had set his mind on a goal, would be relentless in his pursuit of it. My delicate task now was to lure him close to his quarry without allowing him to capture it. Yet he must not abandon the chase or become so discouraged that he sought another lady of the queen's court. I had to remain the object of his desire and yet manage to elude him.

Separation was part of my strategy; while the

king was on progress, hunting with his friends in the shires to the north and west of London, my memory would haunt him, my absence sharpen his desire. I held the advantage, and at summer's end the king would return to court, eager to continue his pursuit of me. Who knew what might happen in the future? I was enjoying the game and not then thinking far ahead.

On the eve of his departure, the king summoned me once again. This time I was prepared. I had dressed in unadorned black damask, and as I was about to follow the king's messenger, I snatched up my rosary and wove the silver beads through my fingers.

"Mademoiselle Anne," said King Henry as I made my three reverences. "Let us converse in French, the language of love."

I was happy to comply. The king often spoke Latin to his courtiers, but I had not been well tutored in Latin and did not speak it easily. French was another thing altogether.

"Tell me, Mademoiselle Anne," said the king. "Have you given thought to our conversation? I confess that you have captured my heart, and I can only hope that I may now claim yours."

"I am flattered by Your Majesty's kindness," I told him. "And I have spent many hours at prayer on the matter." Here I flourished my rosary, piously kissing the cross that hung from it. "I assure Your Majesty that he does now and will always enjoy my deepest affection. But virtue, once lost, cannot be regained."

The king sighed deeply. "God will hear your prayers," he assured me in a voice filled with disappointment, "and will no doubt one day answer mine."

The next morning the king and queen left on progress, and I departed for my parents' estate.

ALTHOUGH I KNEW that I had chosen the right course, I missed the excitement of court and the distractions of the royal progress. Being at Hever always felt like being in exile.

The gardens were overgrown and neglected, and to avoid complete boredom, I engaged several gardeners to work under my direction, trimming back the hedges that had been allowed to grow wild, pruning the roses for a second bloom, and planting beds of pansies with borders of sweet-smelling herbs.

My days were so lacking in diversion that when I received a message from my sister, begging leave to come visit me, I welcomed her. Having few friends among the court ladies, I still counted upon her for gossip and, upon occasion, for companionship.

Mary Carey arrived with a small retinue of her own, including a governess for her daughter, Catherine, a solemn child who seemed to observe the world around her with great seriousness, and a wet nurse for her four-month-old infant son. His name was Henry.

"My daughter named in honor of Queen Catherine, my son in honor of King Henry." Mary smiled, proudly showing off the cooing, gurgling babe with his fringe of reddish gold hair. She must have guessed what I was thinking: *Is it the king's son?* Still, I would not ask, nor did she tell me.

But my sister did provide some astonishing news.

"King Henry has gotten the idea of taking a new wife," she said in a lowered voice, leaning closer. "One young enough to give him the son he wants so badly. I have this on good authority."

"But what of the queen?" I asked, greatly surprised. "Is it possible for him simply to put her aside?"

"My husband tells me that the king intends to obtain a decree of nullity from the church. Will learned this from someone highly placed in Cardinal Wolsey's household, who overheard it from the king's own lips. It is a matter of proving that the marriage was not valid in the first place, and King Henry is now convinced that it was not. Here is his reasoning: Catherine was first married to the king's elder brother, Prince Arthur. But Arthur died only months after the wedding. Six years later Prince Henry wed Arthur's widow. Henry was just seventeen, Catherine twenty-four. Within a month of their marriage, they were crowned king and queen of England."

"I have not heard this story," I said, still much amazed.

"Catherine married Arthur before you were born," Mary reminded me. "Now the king is claiming—so I am told by Will—that a certain verse in the Bible states: If a man takes his brother's wife, it is an unclean thing, and they shall remain childless. King Henry believes that he sinned by marrying Catherine, and now God is punishing him by not allowing him a living son."

"A living *legitimate* son," I said pointedly.

"You are right," Mary agreed, ignoring my bold implication. "Henry Fitzroy lives in royal surroundings in the north of England, but he cannot inherit the throne. And so King Henry has decided to have the pope declare his marriage to Catherine invalid, so that he may marry a new wife."

"Has he such a new wife in mind?" I asked in a carefully neutral tone, determined to conceal the thoughts that were racing through my mind like greyhounds after a stag.

Mary laughed—a little tipsily, I thought, a combination of the spiced wine we'd been drinking and the unusually warm day. "I have no word of that. But I can assure you, Chancellor Wolsey will be the man to guide the king's choice."

"Wolsey!" I burst out with disgust.

"You sound like our father," Mary observed. "He dislikes the cardinal almost as much as you do. But there is nothing to be done about it—Wolsey has been the king's closest adviser since young Prince Henry became King Henry the Eighth seventeen years ago."

Then, turning the conversation in a new direction, she said, "Pity, that Tom Wyatt has no biblical excuse to rid himself of *his* shrew of a wife. I think the poet a fine match for you."

"Pity indeed," I sighed. "I believe that Tom loves me well, and I do care for him." *Not the whole truth,* I thought, *but as much as my sister needs to know.*

That night I couldn't sleep but left my bedchamber to walk alone in the garden beneath a waxing moon. I was thrilled by my sister's claim that the king intended to put aside his wife and take a new one. As my sister and her children slept, I considered how his decision could affect *me.* Until now I had hoped only to win King Henry's heartfelt love and devotion. Each night I paced and pondered, and by the time the moon had reached a silvery fullness and Mary Carey had departed, I was determined to win a much bigger prize. With luck and cleverness I would cause the king to fall so deeply in love with me that he would not rest until he possessed me. But not as his mistress—I would become his wife!

And then a nearly overwhelming truth struck me: If I were King Henry's wife, I would also be his queen.

Queen Anne!

Jubilantly I plucked handfuls of white petals from the full-blooming roses and tossed them high into the silvery moonlight. "Queen Anne! Queen Anne!" I cried. As the petals drifted down around me, I imagined how the cheering throngs would one day call out my name.

CHAPTER 7

# Courtship

## 1526–1527

I had weeks to consider the compelling goals to which I aspired—to marry the king and to become his queen. Then, at last, in early September I left Hever for court. My feelings were a jumble of elation and apprehension. Of one thing I was certain: If I wished the king to wholly lose his heart to me, I must keep my own deepest feelings in check. If I allowed myself to love him too ardently, as ardently as I hoped he'd love me, then I risked surrendering the power to reach my goal. This was a difficult lesson in love that I'd learned long ago by observing the love affairs of the French court.

Now my mother and father settled back into their private apartments at Greenwich Palace, but I was again expected to share the wretched chambers of the queen's maids of honor. Dull as Hever was, I had at least been spared Honor Finch's ceaseless whines and complaints. But it was clear at once that something had happened, and Lady Honor became easy to ignore.

Immense sadness was written upon Queen Catherine's plain, aging face. In public King Henry still treated his wife with great respect, the kind of respect one shows one's mother or a dear sister. He continued to visit her—during the daytime hours—to discuss various matters and to seek her advice. But he no longer came to visit in the evening. Whenever the king entered the queen's chambers, I remained out of sight. I did not want to arouse the queen's jealous suspicions as I had at the Shrovetide jousts.

After my return to Greenwich, I waited each night for the king's summons. There was nothing I could do but wait! Each night when the other maids retired, I stayed up and pretended to read, pleading wakefulness if Honor questioned me. Each morning found me dozing by the dead embers of the fire. A fortnight passed in this manner, and my apprehension grew. *What if he's changed his mind? What if he's found someone else?*

Then, one night as my Bible lay upon my lap, open to the Psalms, the king's messenger arrived with a note from the king. Everyone was asleep—or pretending to be so. In gestures I bade the messenger wait. I woke Nell to help me dress quickly in a simple white kirtle that would bespeak my complete surprise at the summons, and therefore my innocence. My hands trembled so that I could not fasten the jewel I always wore, a diamond on a ribbon about my neck, and Nell did it for me. In a trice I was ready to present myself at the king's most private chamber. "Take this with you," Nell whispered, handing me my Bible. I paused for a moment to calm myself, and then I hurried to the king's chamber.

A single candle guttered on the king's table, where he sat waiting for me. I hesitated for a moment, to let the king drink in the sight of me, shimmering in virginal white. Then I knelt three times, a bit hesitantly this time, apologizing for my poor appearance (it was anything but poor!), protesting that I had been caught unawares by his summons (of course, I had not!). The messenger had vanished. I believed that we were entirely alone.

"Sweetest Anne," said the king, rising, coming closer.

*How tall he is,* I thought as he towered over me. I did observe that he was now considerably heavier than he had been five years earlier, mounted high on his white stallion at the Field of Cloth of Gold. Still, *How strong. How splendid!*

"You cannot imagine how much I have missed you these past weeks," said King Henry. "Every hour without seeing your sweet face seemed like... like an eternity!"

"Your Majesty," I replied, "you have been in my

thoughts as well." I clutched the Bible to my breast and backed away as he reached out for me. "Oh, my lord," I protested, trembling a little, for I was, in truth, somewhat frightened.

"Anne!" he cried, "I have been struck by the dart of love! You have made me weak with desire!"

"I can no longer come to you, Your Majesty," I murmured, my eyes swimming with the tears I summoned. "I will be found out, and my good name will suffer."

"Then, my dearest Anne," said the king gently, "I shall come to you," and he bade me return to my chambers.

THE NEXT DAY my father paid me a visit. I was to be moved out of the maids' chambers and into a private suite with my mother, "by order of King Henry." My father was in a jovial mood, fairly beaming with pride. I was not deluded—it was pride in *himself* that my father displayed, pride that even his less-favored daughter had managed to capture the king's fancy.

But he could not resist lecturing me. "Do whatever it is that His Majesty desires to keep his favor. Do not spoil your chances, whatever you do, by some act of prideful folly."

"I have no intention of spoiling my chances," I assured him. "But I believe that the king respects my intention to preserve my virtue."

"Your virtue!" My father laughed cruelly. "You

can play any game you wish, Nan, just as long as you win."

Even what might have been words of praise from my father ended up poisoned with criticism! Yet much as the harsh words wounded me, I understood that I would need his help.

"I shall need money," I told him.

"I anticipated as much," he said, and laid a leather pouch of coins upon my lap. "Buy whatever you need—jewels, gowns, furs. You have always been good at spending money. Surely there is enough here to satisfy the king's mistress."

"I do not intend to be his mistress," I said coolly.

"Not? Then what is this all about?" I could see the familiar anger flickering in his eyes.

"Have you not heard the rumors, Father? King Henry intends to seek an annulment of his marriage to Queen Catherine and to take a new wife, one who can give him the son he so desires."

"I have heard it."

"I shall become King Henry's wife," I said calmly. "I will bear him not one son, but many." My father stared at me, and I rushed on, boldly stating aloud the intent that had only recently come to me: "And I shall become queen!"

*"Queen!"* my father sneered. "Marry the king! You have always thought overmuch of yourself, daughter, and I see that has not changed."

It was plain that he had no confidence in me. But as he turned to leave, he said, "I assume that I shall hear further from you when you have spent every farthing upon your useless quest." His doubts simply strengthened my resolve to prove him wrong.

IMMEDIATELY I SET about ordering gowns, gloves, slippers, cloaks, hoods, and other items. I impressed upon the silkwomen and embroiderers and glovemakers and furriers the importance of haste, offering them the highest fees in order to have my new wardrobe ready by the Eve of the Feast of the Nativity.

Tom Wyatt continued to play into my plans. One day, as we engaged in some little banter, the poet suddenly grasped a small locket that I wore on a length of lace upon my sleeve and tugged it free. "I fear that you would lose this, madam," he said. "As I have lost my heart to you, and would hope that you have lost yours as well." With that he tucked the locket, lace and all, inside his doublet.

"Sir!" I cried, feigning a little shock and some offense, "what use have you for such a bauble!"

"To wear your pretty locket against my heart," said the poet. "I treasure it as a love token."

I frowned, but I spoke mildly. "Love token? I have given you no love token, sir. You have taken it from me. My heart does not go with it."

KING HENRY seized every opportunity to visit my suite which had a private door easily reached from the king's apartments. Whenever the king arrived, my mother put aside her needlework and tactfully withdrew, leaving us alone and unchaperoned. Sometimes the king came to sup with me, always staying until very late. Every effort was made to keep these visits secret. Even so, by Allhallowtide the whole court was gossiping.

"So," my sister, Mary, whispered one morning in the chapel when we found ourselves kneeling side by side at Mass, "you have decided to take my advice after all and become the king's new mistress!"

"Nothing of the sort," I whispered in reply as we rose for the *Gloria in Excelsis.* "Although the king does continue to flatter me with his kindness."

"But everyone assumes that you have," said Mary. "When you are the king's mistress, you are the center of attention. Enjoy it while you can. From now on every gesture you make, every word you speak, every gown and jewel you wear will be noted. Till now you have been merely a dark-haired maid of no importance. That is past. But beware—you are bound to make enemies...and not just Queen Catherine."

I gasped at her impudence, but I also recognized that she spoke from experience. I tried to shrug off my sister's warning words and set my attention upon the words of the Mass, but a chill of foreboding settled over me.

DURING ONE OF HIS nocturnal visits, the king begged me to give him one of the rings I often wore, a circlet of gold set with a pattern of small diamonds. "As a token of your love," he said.

"As a token of my love," I affirmed, slipping the ring from my own hand and placing it upon his smallest finger. Now Wyatt had a token, and so did the king.

But through all of our many evenings together, King Henry did not say a word of an impending annulment of his marriage. I was resolved that I would not follow in my sister's footsteps and become the king's mistress, but the situation was a dangerous one: If I yielded I would certainly be discarded, as Mary and Bessie had been, but if I continued to refuse him, I risked losing him to someone else—perhaps someone of Wolsey's choosing. And I had to pretend that I knew nothing of his intention to seek an annulment. I slept poorly, and what little I managed to eat lay uneasily upon my stomach. And there was no one in whom I could confide my darkest fears, or my fondest hopes. Most of the maids spoke to me with honeyed words, but I thought them false. Lady Honor and Lady Constance clearly despised me, pointedly ignoring me when I was present, whispering to the others when they didn't know I was nearby: "Why does Anne seem always to dress in black?" I overheard one of the maids, Lady Winifred, ask of Honor.

"Perhaps because she is a crow!" Honor replied, to the amusement of her listeners. *"Caw! Caw!"*

I thought of seeking my mother's counsel, but, although she sometimes advised me on matters of dress and deportment, our hearts were never close. She seemed to enjoy the notion that the second of her daughters had found favor in the king's eyes, but what this might mean in terms of my future was not mentioned.

I did not trust my sister; we had exchanged places, and I believed that she was now jealous of me, as I had once been of her. Mary, I was certain, would simply laugh at me and tell me that I was foolish not to be content with what I had. Fond as I was of Nell, she was but a servant, after all, and perhaps not above sharing secrets with her sister, who served another of the queen's ladies.

The king yearned for me, and yet I was all alone and felt despised.

NEVER HAD THERE BEEN such a Yuletide celebration as the one at the end of 1526. I appeared in my new finery, and at each banquet I danced often with the king. Every eye was upon us.

"Dear lady," King Henry murmured during a gavotte, "if only I could persuade you to be my partner in even more dances! There is no one like you in all this world!"

"Ah, sir, if only!" I replied, my smile sweetly virtuous, my tone of voice hinting at forbidden pleasures.

Sometimes I danced with Tom Wyatt. Tom had

never ceased to pay me court. Tom himself described to me what happened on the day after New Year's when he was playing bowls with King Henry and several of the king's friends. A disagreement arose as to whose bowl had come closest to the jack.

"I drew out the length of lace I always wear about my neck," said Tom, "making sure that the king noticed the jewel hanging upon it—your jewel, dear lady. And I offered to use this as a means to measure the distance. I confess that I could not resist the impulse!"

"Surely, sir, you did no such thing!" I exclaimed, feigning displeasure, but in truth I was well pleased. "Did the king remark upon it?" I asked.

"He did. King Henry recognized it at once as belonging to you. Immediately his mood turned foul. He left the game, muttering oaths. Brandon and the others had no little sport with me after the king had stormed off."

I begged Tom's pardon for any trouble caused him in his friendship with the king, but my words were insincere. The king was jealous, just as I had wished!

TWELFTH NIGHT WAS the last great feast, the climax of the Yuletide season. Wearing a dramatic new gown of black silk, opening upon a white damask petticoat and trimmed with fur, I knew that I had never looked more beautiful. Neither king nor poet could take his eyes off me. For the occasion the king had chosen Tom Wyatt as the Lord of Misrule, whose Lady for the evening would be the one who found the single dried pea baked in the spice cake. Abetted by Nell, who had begged a handful from one of the cooks, I contrived to discover a pea in my slice when the cake was served.

"I am she!" I cried, producing a pea. No one dared dispute my claim, and the Lord of Misrule declared me his lady.

The king was plainly irritated by the attention paid me by Tom, who begged permission to sing a song he had composed.

"Get on with it then," King Henry growled. But no sooner had Tom knelt at my feet with his lute and begun to sing, than the king interrupted. "Enough of this melancholy caterwauling!" he bellowed. "By the king's order, this banquet is at an end!"

The king stalked out, followed dutifully by the queen and their courtiers. Only Princess Mary lingered behind the rest, fixing me with a malevolent stare that I pretended not to notice.

Tom Wyatt took my hand and escorted me from the Great Hall.

"And now I bid you farewell, dearest lady," Tom said, keeping my hand in his.

"Do you not mean 'Good night'?" I asked.

"No, madam; I mean farewell. I leave on the morrow for Italy."

"But you are not gone for long, surely?" I said. "So that you do not forget me."

"Forget you, Lady Anne? Never."

Within days I learned that Tom Wyatt had left for Rome on a diplomatic errand. I guessed the real reason for his leaving: Tom truly loved me, and his departure from England was a sign to the king that he was relinquishing all claims upon my heart.

That winter my loneliness grew. Except for my time with the king, I was always alone among enemies. The maids glowered and whispered among themselves whenever I passed by. *Caw! Caw!* Lady Honor was plainly so jealous that she could scarcely bear to be in the same chamber with me.

"Just look at the sour faces on Lady Honor and Lady Constance!" Nell hissed as she laced up my gown with the French sleeves in the new style I had ordered. "Like they was tasting green apples. And not just them, madam. Everyone's talking!"

The queen's ladies always turned against whoever was chosen by His Majesty. As they now had turned against me.

At the same time, the king began to press harder for me to become his mistress. He became quite open and blunt about his desires, and it was becoming more difficult to refuse him.

"I am a man, Lady Anne! And like other men, I have my appetites that must be satisfied!"

"Your Majesty," I always replied, "you know that you have my deepest affection. But you ask of me what no woman can yield without the loss of her virtue and her self-respect. And, my lord, the loss of *your* respect as well." Then I would lower my eyes and clasp my hands beseechingly.

"No, my love!" the king protested. "Nothing will ever cause me to lose respect for you! I solemnly swear it!"

But such avowals would not persuade me to yield. I would not be swept off my feet and lose every chance to have what I wanted most.

And then one evening everything changed. The great King Henry, the most powerful man in all of England, took my hands in both of his. "Dearest Anne! I love you with all my heart and soul!" he cried. "My deepest desire is to make you mine forever!"

These were words I yearned to hear. Yet in his declaration I heard no proposal of marriage, no mention of an annulment of his present marriage, without which there could be no new marriage to me. I had begun to despair that *my* deepest desires—to be his wife and his queen—might go unmet.

"My lord," I replied carefully. "Unworthy as I am, you honor me with your deep affection."

"Then be mine, as I am yours!"

"But you know that I cannot, my lord, as much as I may wish it." Honest tears gathered in my eyes, and I could not stop them from spilling over. The king embraced me.

King Henry's voice seemed choked with regret as he finally explained his unhappy predicament. "Before God, Anne, it is my belief that my marriage to the queen is not now and has never been valid. It was an error that I humbly and sincerely regret and now must do whatever is necessary to correct. I have sinned against God's law, and I am being punished for it. God has given me no sons."

At last he had brought up the subject of his invalid marriage! "Oh, my poor friend," I murmured, leaning against his broad chest as my tears flowed freely, "is there no solution?"

Still holding me close, the king explained that for some time he had been consulting with the theologians of his court. "Only the pope in Rome has the power to dissolve this marriage," said the king. "But it must be done." Abruptly he released me and began to pace restlessly about his chamber, pounding his fist into his palm. "It must be done! It must!"

THROUGHOUT THE MONTHS that followed, talk of the annulment never failed to excite the king. At times he was jubilant, certain that the theologians he had charged with presenting his case would persuade the pope. At other times King Henry gave way to dejection. Mostly, though, he was impatient.

I recognized that my position was very dangerous. There was still no marriage proposal, and I worried that Chancellor Wolsey might already be busily promoting some other royal match. With one slight miscalculation, or one stroke of ill luck, everything could come to ruin.

## CHAPTER 8

# George

## 1527

As it happened, the person now closest to me was my brother, George. No longer the spoiled little boy who'd shouted and stamped his foot, he was now a man of eighteen, newly married to Jane Parker, a lady with an imperious air who made clear her disdain for me.

As my father's fortunes improved, so had my brother's. George had risen from the lowly position of page to become one of the king's cupbearers. His duty was to hold the golden goblet to the king's mouth when he dined, taking care that no drops of wine fell upon the king's rich clothing. Being so often close to the king's lips, he heard much of what the king had to say. Charming and well made, George had also earned a name as a poet, and now that Tom Wyatt was gone, George's verses were in even greater demand. Late in January of 1527, I invited him to call upon me in private.

"So," said my brother, taking his ease in my chamber and calling for a flagon of ale, "you have caught the king's fancy, as our sister once did. You are the talk of the court, Nan."

"True enough that I have caught the king's fancy," I replied, "but not as our sister did."

"Meaning—?"

"Meaning that I have refused to become his mistress."

"Refused to become the king's mistress? What then, Nan?"

I hesitated. "You must speak of this to no one," I said, thinking of his wife, whom I did not trust.

"You have my solemn word," he said, raising his hand and regarding me now with great seriousness.

I leaned close to him. "I intend to become the king's wife."

"His *wife*?" George laughed heartily, displaying his strong white teeth. "You would be the king's *wife*?"

"If it be God's will and the king's pleasure, I shall marry King Henry."

"I know naught of God's will, but I can tell you this much: King Henry is in love. He talks of you constantly and of how he has been struck by the dart of love. You hold his heart in your own two hands."

"Much as did our sister."

"The king was entranced by our sister's body," said George crudely. "It is your whole person that entrances him. But *marriage*? That is another thing entirely. Ambitious as our father may be, we are not highborn. And there is the unavoidable fact that the king already has a wife."

"But King Henry intends to have his marriage nullified."

George nodded. "I have heard as much. Apparently, he views it as a matter of conscience. There is a problem, though—I have heard him speak of it."

"And that is—?" I waited anxiously to hear my brother's reply.

"The pope, who must grant the decree of nullity, was appointed by Emperor Charles. The emperor is Catherine's nephew and will not allow his aunt to be put aside easily. The queen will certainly oppose the annulment, and the emperor will take up her cause with the pope. This will not be a simple thing, dear sister."

"But the king loves me, does he not? He will triumph in the end, will he not?"

"Yes, Nan, the king loves you. And he is not used to being refused. I know that he will do everything in his power to get what he wants. And he plainly wants *you*."

"Then I shall be queen!" I said.

"Queen?" George stared at me, astounded. "Your ambition knows no bounds! Would you not be content simply to be the king's wife and consort?"

"No," I said. "I would be queen."

I waited to see if he would sneer at me as our father had. But George raised his flagon in a toast. "Then I drink to the future Queen Anne," he said, smiling broadly, "for that will make me the king's brother-in-law."

THE ENTIRE COURT was engaged in a frenzy of preparation for a festive event to take place in April: the betrothal of young Princess Mary to François, king of France. This was the same François of whose court I had been a member, and the same François whose wife, Queen Claude, I had once served. But Claude had died, and François was now ready to take a new wife. Evidently King Henry had decided that betrothing his daughter to the French monarch would be to his advantage.

Such events were months in the planning. I ordered several new gowns, and the talk among Queen Catherine's ladies was of nothing but the coming celebration. There was gossip that the princess was anything but pleased by the marriage arrangements made for her by her father, and she had treated her seamstresses to more than one royal outburst. François was thirty-three years old, three years younger than King

Henry, but I'm sure Princess Mary, just eleven, thought of him as hopelessly old and drooling, like her aunt Mary Brandon's French king.

It was a spring of violent storms, and the arrival of the French entourage was delayed for three weeks until the crossing from Calais could be made safely. When at last the skies cleared and the seas calmed, word was received that François and his great retinue of courtiers and servants had landed in Dover. Escorted by a band of knights and henchmen displaying the Tudor colors, the visitors made their way to Greenwich, where Princess Mary and her sour-faced governess, the countess of Salisbury, had been waiting grumpily for over a month.

On the feast day honoring Saint George, patron saint of England, King Henry and Queen Catherine gave a great banquet to welcome the French. Although five years had passed since I'd left his court and returned to England, François singled me out for special greetings. As he bent over my hand, François murmured in French, "And how fares your sister, Mademoiselle Marie?"

I explained that "Marie," now Mary Carey, was the contented mother of two and spent less time at court.

"And you are following in the footsteps of that great courtesan, are you not, Mademoiselle Anne?" he asked. "I understand that King Henry has a great fondness for you. He shows himself to be a man of exquisite taste." François winked broadly.

"I am the king's loyal subject, and the queen's," I replied with a deep curtsy. François merely smiled, bowing gallantly.

Three days later Princess Mary, lost in her heavy robes and ornate jewels, was pledged to the king of France. At the banquet that followed in honor of the newly betrothed couple, a masque was performed to entertain the French king and his courtiers. I was one of the dancers, as was the princess. As the master of revels rehearsed us in the steps of the dance, I was aware of the princess peering at me shortsightedly. I wondered if someone—the queen, perhaps?—had spoken to her of me, but then I realized that the king's attentions to me were so transparent that the child could see for herself that her father was in love with me. When I became the king's wife, she would be my stepdaughter; I guessed that it would not be an easy association.

During the time of the French visit, the king had fewer opportunities than usual to come to my apartments. It was mid-May before Princess Mary and her governess departed for distant Ludlow, where the princess kept her own household, and François sailed for France.

The day after their departure, my brother brought me a report of the latest court gossip. "Prepare yourself for a rival, Nan."

"Rival? Of whom do you speak, brother?"

"Princess Renée of France, a cousin of François."

My old friend, Princess Renée, to be my rival? "I

have not heard of this," I said, trying to recall when I had last exchanged letters with Renée.

"You are hearing of it now. The match is the idea of your great champion, Cardinal Wolsey."

"My champion!" I spat furiously. "I will see that 'champion' in his grave!"

"You may, indeed, dear sister," said George agreeably, and he rose to take his leave.

When he had gone, I paced restlessly about my chamber. *Princess Renée! Wolsey!* In a rage I seized George's empty tankard and flung it against the wall. The metallic clatter caused Nell to rush in. She found me dissolved in bitter tears.

THAT NIGHT King Henry stormed into my apartments and flung himself into his chair, one of the few chairs in the palace and kept there for his sole use.

"Outrage!" he shouted, and barked orders at Nell to fetch him two dozen oysters. When she had hurried away to do his bidding, King Henry sat with his head in his hands. He looked weary and overburdened. Then he managed a smile and beckoned.

"Come, sweetheart, and sit with me."

Obediently, I permitted him to draw me upon his knees, a liberty that I had recently begun to allow. "Has all not gone well, Your Majesty?" I asked.

"What cunning deceivers, those French!" he said. "The king's ambassadors met with me as they were preparing to leave, and, after all that I had done for them, the lengths to which I had gone to entertain them, you cannot imagine what they said!"

"Tell me, my lord," I urged.

"They have refused to agree to a wedding! They say that perhaps in another three or four years, when Princess Mary has become a woman, she will be fit for marriage and childbearing. The insult!" The king pushed me from his lap and began to pace from one end of my chamber to the other. The space was too small to contain the king and his wrath. Even the prompt arrival of the oysters did little to soothe him.

"That is not all," announced King Henry. "I ordered Wolsey to convene a secret court with representatives from the pope in order to obtain an annulment of my marriage to Catherine, but the queen learned of my intent. Now she protests her undying love for me—for that she may be forgiven—but she refuses to admit that our marriage is not valid and never has been. She argues with me! She points out that if the marriage is invalid, then our daughter is made a bastard."

*And what of Princess Renée?* I ached to ask, but I dared not.

"'So be it,' I told her," King Henry continued, his face growing red. "'Mary is a jewel, the pearl of the world, but she is still only a woman and unfit to rule, no matter whom she marries. I must have sons!' I was reasonable; Catherine was not. She will have none of it. I cannot understand her stubbornness. The queen is an intelligent woman! I respect her judgment in many things. But she has determined not to agree with me in this."

"But you are right, Your Majesty," I assured him, concealing my deep concerns, "and the queen is wrong. Her Majesty may argue all she pleases, but in the end the pope will surely accept your reasoning, and Queen Catherine will be forced to accept his judgment."

My calming words eventually restored the king to good temper, he called for more oysters, and so the evening ended peacefully. But worse news was soon to follow: Emperor Charles had ordered the sack of Rome, and Pope Clement had fled into exile. For the time being, the pope could do nothing for the king. But neither could the cardinal do anything about Princess Renée.

THROUGH ALL OF THIS, I was challenged to continue to play my role as maid of honor to the queen. I was constantly in Catherine's presence. She didn't send me away, as well she might have. How odd it seemed—my days were spent in the company of the queen and my nights in the company of the king, her husband. I was a player in two different masques and lived constantly with the fear that I would make a misstep with one or the other. The fear disturbed my rest. I worried that lack of sleep would take its toll on my appearance, although Nell reassured me that I had lost none of my allure.

One day in early summer, the queen summoned

me to a card game, as she sometimes did. On that occasion I was unusually lucky. *Perhaps it is a sign,* I thought, as I discarded two of the last three cards in my hand and prepared to sweep up my winnings.

The queen said tartly, "So, Lady Anne, you have discarded the valet and the chevalier but not the king! You continue to hold him fast in your hand. You will, it seems, have all!" She rose abruptly, nearly knocking over the table, and all of us leaped to our feet as well. "You are dismissed, Lady Anne," she said.

I was still the queen's subject, bound to obey her. I felt the blood rush to my face as I knelt and then left the queen's chamber in haste.

As summer approached, I decided that the wisest course was to retire once again to my family's home at Hever—the better to tantalize the king with my absence and the better to avoid the queen's icy stares. The night before the king and queen were to leave on summer progress, King Henry appeared in my apartments, seeming even more agitated than usual. I wondered if he had received more unwelcome news.

For an hour or more he paced restlessly. He called for oysters but didn't eat them. He called for ale but didn't drink it. He talked about the progress on which he would depart in the morning, the noble families he would visit, the hunting he looked forward to. I listened quietly and waited, concealing my own agitation.

Suddenly he stopped his pacing and gazed at me. He looked pale, and beads of sweat stood out on his forehead. *Is he ill?* I wondered. And then he dropped to his knees and knelt before me. I stifled a cry, for I had seen the king kneel only before God's altar in the chapel royal.

"Marry me, dearest Anne!" he cried, as though his heart would burst. "Promise that you will be my wife!"

I caught my breath, feeling light-headed. *It is happening,* I thought, *just as I had hoped!* I, too, fell to my knees. "Unworthy as I am, Your Majesty, I could ask for nothing more than to be your devoted wife," I told him. As we knelt together and King Henry's kisses covered my face, I exulted: *I shall be the king's wife!*

Later, when the king had gone and I was alone, I began to dance. Around my chamber I danced my joy, leaping and gliding, inventing my own steps to the thrilling music that sang in my mind and my heart: *I shall be queen! I shall be the king's wife, and I shall be queen!*

## CHAPTER 9

# Engagement

## *1527–1528*

"I shall need additional moneys," I informed my father soon after my return to Hever in July. "The king has proposed marriage." I waited to see what effect my announcement would have.

Thomas Boleyn glanced up from a letter he was writing and frowned at me. "It is a poor jest that you make, daughter."

"It is no jest, Father. King Henry wishes me to become his wife. I must dress the part."

"It is common knowledge that the king intends to set aside the queen," he said, eyebrows raised in doubt. "What makes you think that he means to have *you* as his wife?"

"I am certain of it," I replied proudly. I showed

him a bracelet fashioned of gold with the king's likeness set in a medallion. "A gift from the king," I said, "delivered by the king's messenger this very day. And this, as well." I handed him a letter.

*I and my heart put ourselves in your hands,* the letter began, in French, and continued with many loving words. *Since I cannot be with you in person, I send you the nearest thing possible, my likeness set in a bracelet, wishing myself in its place. This from the hand of your loyal servant, H. Rex*

What a pleasure, to have the upper hand in the presence of my usually scornful father! "Plainly, King Henry cannot approach you to arrange a betrothal so long as his marriage to Queen Catherine is valid," I said. "But that matter will soon be finished."

My father leaned on his elbows, making an arch of his fingers. "I have also heard, on good authority, that the pope is in no position to grant the nullity."

"Must you always think the worst?" I asked impatiently. "Surely you know that the king has sent Chancellor Wolsey with a retinue numbering more than a thousand to Calais. He intends to bring about peace between France and the emperor, and so restore Pope Clement to his rightful place. Then the king's annulment will proceed without further hindrance." I jingled the bracelet. "And now," I continued, "I wish to send the king a token."

The next day my father delivered another sack of coins to me.

I had already described the design to the royal goldsmith: a little ship made of pure gold, with the tiny figure of a woman standing on the deck, the whole to be set with a large diamond. "With all haste," I told the smith, counting out the coins.

Within a fortnight the small treasure was finished. Recalling my childhood voyage to Calais, I sent it to the king along with this brief message: *How like this maiden I am, tossed about by stormy seas, at the mercy of fate and Your Majesty's will.*

Soon I had from the king a letter expressing pleasure and thanks for my gift and enclosing another token, a love knot wrought of gold. While the king's letters were always filled with deep yearning (*Consider well, my dearest love, how greatly my absence from you grieves me. . . .*), I took care in my replies to reveal far less of my heart. The king must not be allowed to become too sure of my love, lest he tire of a prize too easily won.

The ardent letters and the king's gifts continued to arrive throughout the summer. *Would you were in my arms or I in yours, for I think it long since I kissed you,* he wrote, and then described to me a hart he'd killed while out that day with his hunting party. He signed his letter, *by the hand of him who shortly shall be yours. H.R.*

WITH THE COMING of autumn, I sensed a change, although my daily life proceeded as before. The king returned from his hunting progress, and my mother and I took up our residence once more at Greenwich Palace. I resumed my service as maid of honor to the queen, who pretended that I did not exist. The ladies of the court stopped talking when I entered, staring at me and making no effort to conceal their contempt. At banquets in the Great Hall, Queen Catherine took her customary place by the king's side, smiling graciously as though nothing in her royal world had been shaken. But beneath the courtly behavior, tumultuous feelings seethed.

Then Wolsey returned from Calais. I could well imagine the anger—the fury!—that would overtake the cardinal when he learned of the king's decision to make me his wife.

I employed sweet reason to keep at bay the king's desire, which had grown even stronger during our separation. "Soon we shall be man and wife," I told him. "Our marriage bed will be blessed, I promise you, and you will father many sons. But we must wait. I say this not from a selfish need to protect my reputation but from the need to protect the future of the throne. Would you risk having another bastard son, Your Majesty?"

"Ah, sweetheart, you are right," the king agreed reluctantly.

I smiled at him winsomely. "Our day will come, my lord," I said. "And our nights as well."

In fact, I no longer had even a shred of reputation to protect. King Henry made no secret of his passion for me, and the entire court believed I had long since become his mistress.

Among the many gifts the king lavished upon me was a handsome gray palfrey with an elegant saddle and finely wrought trappings. There was also a beautiful falcon with an exquisitely embroidered leather glove, upon which the bird had been trained to perch, and a soft hood to cover her until she was ready to hunt. I was eager to try out my pretty little merlin. But on my first invitation to hunt with the king, I showed that I was not skilled at hawking, and King Henry proved an impatient tutor.

"Princess Mary hunts exceptionally well," he informed me. "Perhaps I should have my daughter instruct you in the fine art of falconry.

I was incensed by his remark. Without thinking, I snapped, "Perhaps I should then instruct your daughter the princess in ways to enchant a French suitor."

I was horrified at my own bold words, but there was no way to call them back. The king seemed stunned that anyone dared to speak to him in such a manner. We stared at each other, and my mind raced in search of a proper sort of apology. But the king burst into laughter so hearty that the rest of the hunting party turned to see the cause of the merriment.

"My sweetheart is as high-spirited as her palfrey!" he roared. "A tongue as sharp as a rapier is a fine weapon for a lady, provided she does not draw more blood than she intends!"

I smiled. Clearly, the king enjoyed my quick wit,

but I resolved that I must keep it in careful check, as I did the little palfrey.

I LOOKED FORWARD eagerly to the coming Yuletide season. My father, observing the esteem in which the king now held me—esteem that reflected well upon Thomas Boleyn—saw to it that I had all the moneys I needed to order the wardrobe necessary to my new and more public role: a gown of tawny velvet trimmed with black lambs' fur, another of russet silk, two in black velvet, one in white satin with crimson sleeves, a robe of purple cloth of gold lined with silver, thirteen kirtles, eight embroidered nightgowns, three cloaks furred with miniver, and two dozen pairs of black velvet slippers.

In acknowledgment of my place as the most important lady at court—save for the queen—and in the king's heart, my father presented me with a lovely jewel, the letter *B* set with diamonds, to wear upon a ribbon about my neck. I recognized that my father intended the jewel to be a reminder to King Henry of the notability of the Boleyn family. My father was using the king's obvious love for me as a way to increase his own power and influence.

Yet in the midst of all the attention being paid to me in that first autumn of King Henry's open courtship, I was often unbearably lonely. There was no one with whom I could share the simple pleasures of my new life. When I was not in the king's company, I was alone, except for occasional visits from George. No matter where I went, all talk ceased and all eyes turned to glare at me. I had the king's love. But at the Yuletide banquets Catherine still sat by his side on the royal dais. Princess Mary, who'd been moved from distant Ludlow Castle to Richmond Palace, west of London, shot me hateful looks. Everyone at court had heard that the king intended to leave his wife and marry me. And they despised me for it.

The ladies who sat with their needlework also embroidered their stories about me. The card players placed bets that I would not stay long in the king's favor. They whispered about the blemish upon my neck and the budding sixth finger. The ladies—including my sister-in-law, Jane Boleyn—spoke to me only when compelled by the customs of the court.

It was a different story with the gentlemen. They were drawn by my dark looks, my witty conversation, my laughter, the hint of danger and enticement that clung to me like an exotic perfume. They hovered about me, vying for my attention, but I trusted these gentlemen no more than I trusted their wives.

Yet whom *could* I trust? My family was loyal to me, certainly, tied by bonds of blood, but, with the exception of my brother, George, I felt close to none of them. My sister was jealous of me; my mother advised me not to make too much of the king's attentions; my father only wanted to use me for his own gains and seemed to dislike me. The answer, always, was that I was truly alone.

KING HENRY SENT ME a handsome ruby ring, but there was no invitation to join him and the queen and the princess and his court favorites for the exchange of gifts on New Year's Day. I knew the reason—my presence would have offended his wife and daughter—and I resented it.

"Never again!" I cried angrily to my mother. "Never again will the old queen occupy what the king means to be *my* place!"

"Perhaps you are wrong about that, dear Nan," my mother replied in her mild voice. "The king may speak of his love for you, but it is still Queen Catherine who sits beside him."

"What can I do? The king promises that he will soon be free to marry, but—"

"But," my mother interrupted, "perhaps you are asking for too much. You already have the king's favor."

I took from my mother the book she'd been reading, closed it, and laid it aside. Then I knelt at her feet and clasped her two hands in mine. "What is it that you suggest, Mother?" I asked.

She stared down at our joined hands. "Become the king's mistress," she said softly. "As your sister once did. Is it not better to know that you have the king's ardent love, and to settle for that, than to risk losing all by continuing to refuse what he asks of you?"

I let go her hands and rose to my feet. "I shall have all," I stated flatly.

"Then it is all or nothing?"

"It is not a question of 'all or nothing,' Mother. I mean to have *all.*"

THROUGHOUT THE WINTER, I waited. King Henry continued to visit my apartments as frequently as ever and to flatter me with gifts, including an emerald ring and a love knot cunningly set with diamonds and rubies. In February my father was made an earl by the king, and thus my mother became a countess. Both were quite pleased by their higher standing at court.

And still I waited.

On May Day the members of the court gathered on Shooter's Hill, near Greenwich Palace. A rustic banqueting chamber had been erected, the walls covered with flowers and sweet-smelling herbs. The king, disguised as Robin Hood, arrived in the company of two hundred archers dressed in green velvet. When the banqueting had ended, "Robin Hood" summoned the master of the hounds, who presented me with a pair of excellent greyhounds, to be taken on the summer hunting progress.

A week later King Henry called me to his privy chamber. He had good news: The pope, who had managed to escape from captivity, had granted authority to Cardinal Wolsey and an Italian cardinal, Campeggio, to hear arguments and to make a judgment concerning the king's marriage. The king was elated, confident that the judgment would go in his favor.

"It is not too soon to begin planning our wedding, sweetheart," he said. This was the first time he had used the word *wedding*! "I expect to have the nullity granted in a matter of weeks, and then we shall be wed."

Like any happy young bride, I rushed to tell my mother. She was delighted to help me with designs for what I determined would be an occasion of unrivaled magnificence. The only event I could imagine that would surpass my wedding would be my coronation as queen.

CHAPTER 10

# Fatal Illness

## 1528–1529

The king was wrong. The weeks passed with no encouraging word of an annulment; Cardinal Campeggio seemed in no hurry to make the journey from Rome. Then we received frightening news that eclipsed all other concerns: An outbreak of the sweating sickness was sweeping through London. Many had died.

Dr. Butts, the royal physician, first raised the alarm. "The sweating sickness has scourged London three times in the past," he reminded us, "each time claiming more lives than the time before."

As our awareness grew of the rapid advance of this terrible illness, our fear grew as well. The sweating sickness had no cure. It struck down its victims with awful swiftness, taking the lives of the strong, the youthful, and the hale, leaving behind the weak, the old, and the sickly, as though they were beneath the notice of the Angel of Death. Few would be left to tend the dying and dispose of the dead. But London, a city of seventy thousand souls, was a few miles upriver from Greenwich. Perhaps, I thought, the scourge would pass us by. It did not.

"It is the punishment for our sins!" cried Nell, rushing into my apartments with the news: Several servants in the king's scullery, one of the royal apothecaries, four or five of the attendants in the king's chambers, and Nell's own sister had been stricken with the sweats. "Mistress, they are already dead!" she wailed.

"And the king?" I asked, trying to rise but already faint with dread.

Nell shook her head, burst into tears, and fled. I hastened after her, not knowing if her sobs meant that the king, too, had been stricken.

My flight was intercepted by my brother, George. "Come, Nan," he said, seizing my hand, which was cold and trembling. "Let us return to your apartments. I have a letter for you from the king."

He called for a servant to fetch us wine. There was no response. The servants had all disappeared. "What is happening?" I said, weeping. "Where is the king?"

"He has gone to his manor house in Essex,"

George replied, "in order to escape the poisonous vapors."

"The king is gone?" I asked, my lips quivering.

"He is the king, and he must preserve his own life before any of ours. Surely you understand that, Nan?"

"Yes, I understand," I murmured. *But if he truly loves me, why did he leave me? Why did he not take me with him?*

I broke the seal on the king's letter. The writing was not in King Henry's own hand but that of another; the letter was merely a list of precautions to be taken if one hoped to escape the illness. The king had ordered that live coals be kept burning in braziers in every chamber, and vinegar sprinkled about liberally. We were advised to eat and drink sparingly, to avoid the company of large numbers of people, and to try not to give way to fear. At the end the king had added his own scrawl, *"Be of good comfort, cherished sweetheart. H.R."*

I crumpled the letter and tossed it away distractedly as I paced about the chamber, suddenly gripped by dread—fear for the king foremost, but also fear for my own fate. "Suppose he dies, George! Then Princess Mary inherits the throne, and Queen Catherine rules in her stead until Mary is of age. Can you imagine my life if Catherine rules and King Henry is no longer here to protect me? She will make my life a living—"

I stopped abruptly when I saw that my brother had slumped over the table, clutching his head. "George!" I cried, shaking him. He made no reply. His eyes were open, but he saw nothing. Perspiration was soaking through his doublet, giving off a foul odor. My brother had the sweating sickness!

Sobbing, I called out for help, but no one came. With great effort I tugged his limp body off the table where he had collapsed and attempted to drag him into my bedchamber, but he was far too heavy for me. Bringing a pillow for his head, I tried to make him comfortable where he lay, although he seemed past awareness of either comfort or misery. Although the day was warm, he had begun to shiver violently. I heaped coverlets upon him, wiped his face with my handkerchief dipped in a bit of water left in a flagon, and set out once again to find help.

It began as a little pain in my head and a weakness in my legs as I hurried through the gallery to the Great Hall, where I hoped to find servants or an apothecary or anyone at all who could come to my brother's aid. Quickly the pain grew much stronger, and my legs much weaker. I cried out as I fell to the floor, unable to move, unable even to think. I remember a mangy dog coming to snuffle at my face. After that, I remember nothing at all.

MY MOTHER LATER described to me what had happened. George and I were both found, more dead than alive, by guards who recognized us. The guards summoned an assistant to the royal astrologer, who arranged to have us transported by litter all the way to Hever. My father, similarly stricken, was brought to Hever soon after. I know not how many days I languished there, life ebbing and flowing like the tides in the River Thames.

"The priest administered the last rites to all three of you," my mother told me as she sat by my bedside when at last it seemed likely that I would live. "I did not expect any of you to survive, despite my ceaseless prayers."

"And the king?" I asked weakly. "Has there been some word from him?"

"There has. When he learned of your illness, King Henry sent Dr. Butts to minister to you. This he did, preparing an herbal plaster, favored by the king himself, to draw out the poisons from your body. He fed you concoctions made of herbs and ginger mixed with wine—do you remember none of this, Nan?—but the good doctor could only tell me, as he tells everyone, 'There is nothing more to be done for the patient but to pray.' "

All of us did survive, but my poor mother was in a state of exhaustion. Many of our servants had either died of the terrible disease or were still weakened themselves.

Then a royal messenger delivered a letter sealed with the king's insignia. With trembling hands I broke it open.

*The uneasiness caused me by my doubts about your*

*health have much disturbed and alarmed me,* the king had written. *Therefore I beg of you, my beloved, to have no fear or to be uneasy at our separation, for wherever I am, I am wholly yours.* At the end of the letter King Henry had drawn a heart enclosing my initials and placed his own, H.R., on either side of the heart. I smiled and touched my lips to the heart.

My mother took the letter from me as I fell back upon my pillows. "I trust it is good news?" she asked.

"He loves me still," I said, drifting off to sleep once more.

It was at this time of great danger to all, from mighty king to lowliest pauper, that I first truly realized the depth of my feeling for King Henry. What had begun as a game and become a goal had grown into genuine love on my part as well as his.

DAILY WE RECEIVED news of more sickness and death. Among those who had not survived was Lady Honor Finch; I managed a brief prayer for the repose of her wretched soul. Nell had fallen ill but recovered; the lad to whom she was betrothed was not so fortunate. I had not yet left my bedchamber when we received the sad news that Will Carey had fallen victim, and my widowed sister was beside herself with sorrow.

"She knows not what to do or where to turn," my mother said. "She trusts that we will help her."

I was still very weak when Mary arrived at Hever with her two young children, looking so haggard and bent with care that I scarcely recognized her. Her condition touched my heart. Leaning upon each other for support, we walked slowly to the sunny bower where three years earlier we had talked together. Mary had spoken blithely then of the king's infatuation that had resulted in his naming a ship for her. How low she had fallen since. My sister was now a widow with fading looks, two children, and no prospects.

"I am desperate, Nan," she confided tearfully. "I have no money; William left nothing but gambling debts." She raised her great blue eyes to meet mine, pleading. "I have no way to pay them, save to pawn my few jewels. Unless you can help me," she added, lowering her eyes once more.

Perhaps it was my own frailty that caused me to respond as I did. My gaze drifted from my sister to the two children playing nearby. The little girl, Catherine, looked much like her mother. As for the boy, I could have sworn that I saw the likeness of the king in the sturdy little fellow. This ignited the old jealousy that had smoldered since childhood.

"This is none of my affair," I said coldly. "I cannot help you."

If I had expected tears, or pleading for the children's sake, or promises to repay me, I was entirely wrong. Mary erupted in a rage. "You!" she cried so loudly that both children stopped in their little game and stared at us, mouths agape. "You have always been the most selfish of women! You cannot use lack of money as an excuse not to help your own needful sister, for I know that you are the king's mistress, as I once was, and I know that he has showered you with gifts of great value, as he once did me. But I've had to sell most of those gifts for a small part of their worth to pay my husband's debts and now to care for my fatherless children. Yet you have so little true feeling in your heart that you refuse to help your own good sister who suffers in the most direful need!"

Her words incensed me. "For shame, Mary! You dare speak to me like that? You traded your virtue and your reputation for pretty jewels and boasted that the king named a ship for you! The wonder is that your poor husband put up with you for all that time."

For a moment I thought she was going to slap me, as she often had when we were children. But the rage vanished as quickly as it had come, and my sister threw herself at my feet, sobbing as though her heart were breaking. "But I loved him! I loved him more than you could ever understand, for your heart is made of ice!"

Her fervor surprised me. "You speak of William Carey?"

"I speak of King Henry! I adored him for the man that he is, and I gave myself to him out of the love that overflowed my heart. Not like you, Nan! You want to marry the king only to become queen—*not because you love him*!"

Her words cut me to the quick. "You are wrong,

Mary," I said quietly. "I love him well." My hands dropped limply into my lap. "And the child?" I asked, nodding toward the boy who stood at a little distance, staring at his mother. "Who is the father?"

"I know not," she whispered. "My husband was Will Carey, but the man I loved was King Henry. Both made claims upon me."

Overcome with remorse at my harsh words, I reached out my arms, and the child moved slowly toward me, thoughtfully chewing his lip.

"Come, my poppet," I coaxed. "Let us find the cook and see if she has a sweet confit for you." The boy looked at me searchingly for a moment, then placed his hand in mine. Little Henry made his decision and came away with me. As he did so, I turned to my sister. "Of course, I will help you, Mary," I said. "And your children as well."

KING HENRY RETURNED from his country manor, where he had escaped the perils of the sweating sickness, and called me to join him. Our reunion was a joyous one, as he had promised, and there were more pretty gifts: silver bindings for my favorite books. True to my promise to Mary, I asked the king to make me the guardian of little Henry Carey, and he willingly granted my request.

King Henry seemed more high-spirited than ever, brimming with confidence that soon he would be rid of his wife, the queen, by action of the pope or of the pope's representative, Campeggio, and we would soon be wed. The king was so certain of the validity of his claim that he refused to consider that he might lose.

With the queen away from court at her manor house in Hertfordshire, the king no longer felt any constraint in publicly showing his great affection for me. We were constantly in each other's company, exchanging kisses and fond touches and endearments. To amuse ourselves, we exchanged love notes in the chapel royal during the Mass. Henry passed me his book of hours, where he had written on a blank page,

> *If you remember my love in your prayers as strongly as I adore you, I shall hardly be forgotten. I am yours forever.*
>
> *HR*

Before the Mass had ended, I added my own lines and returned the book to the king.

> *By daily proof you shall me find*
> *To be to you both loving and kind.*

On those occasions when we were apart for even a few days, the king wrote me passionate letters expressing his longing for me. Our happy future seemed almost close enough to grasp.

I was even in a mood to forgive my archenemy, Wolsey, should he bring the matter of the king's annulment to a speedy and happy conclusion. Perhaps it would mean a happy ending even for Catherine, who could withdraw to a convent and spend her life in contemplation and prayer, a role that suited her far better than being wife to a man like King Henry VIII!

AT LAST WE RECEIVED word that Cardinal Campeggio was on his way from Rome by way of Paris. Soon all would be settled. To avoid any accusation of impropriety from this Italian prelate, my mother and I withdrew to Hever, where I would occupy myself in planning the royal wedding. I had to order my gown and choose the designs for the maids and pages who would attend me. There were many other details: the list of guests; the banquets; the arrangements for the chapel royal, where Cardinal Wolsey himself would celebrate the Mass!

But after a few weeks at Hever, I received a visit from George. "Dear Nan," he said, "I urge you to return to London at once. It is apparent to me that, without your presence, the king loses determination. His advisers, particularly Wolsey, urge him to find an easier course, and I fear that he may come to agree."

My mood of forgiveness toward Wolsey vanished. I could well imagine the chancellor's advice to King Henry: *Think of Princess Renée! A marriage with her would strengthen our ties with France, and the princess is just as able as Lady Anne to provide the sons you need!*

"We are returning to London," I informed my

mother, and within days we had taken up residence at Bridewell Palace.

When the king did not come to me at once, I began to fret that Wolsey's poisonous advice was having its effect. Worry shortened my temper and roughened my tongue. "I rarely see you!" I complained on one of the infrequent occasions when the king dared to visit me. "What way is this to treat the woman you wish to marry?"

"Ah, sweetheart mine, have patience, I beg you!" the king implored. "We must behave properly so long as Campeggio lurks about, his ear filled with the pleadings of the queen and her supporters."

*And your ears filled with Wolsey's!* I fumed silently. "Can you not put a stop to those pleadings?" I cried. "Are you not the king? Have you no say in this matter?"

My intemperate words took King Henry by surprise, and I saw that I had gone too far. "Enough!" he roared. "I will put up with no more of your complaints, madam."

The king's fierce temper was well-known. I had often witnessed its power when he unleashed it against a clumsy courtier or a hapless servant. But this was the first time I had felt the heat of it directed at me, and it frightened me. I fell immediately to my knees, begging forgiveness, claiming that it was only my love for him and my desire to be his wife that had given my tongue such sharpness. He forgave me, but I quickly realized two things: The king's will could be easily undermined by others, and I'd best keep a tight rein on my own temper, for the king's patience with me clearly had its limits.

CARDINAL CAMPEGGIO did not convene the tribunal to hear the king's case until the end of May—nine months after his arrival in England. Again King Henry urged me to return to Hever, for the sake of propriety. I was reluctant to leave him, but I dared not refuse.

I heard about the queen's dramatic appearance before the tribunal not from King Henry, but from my brother, who had been in a position to observe. "Queen Catherine was present," George reported, "as was the king, who sat on a great throne. The queen defended herself so well from the king's accusations that her supporters—and she has a great many—cheered her with enthusiasm."

"It matters not in the least what Catherine's supporters want," I reminded him. "The tribunal will decide."

## CHAPTER 11

# In the Queen's Place

## *1529–1530*

As Nell was helping me dress, King Henry burst into my apartments. His face was red, and a great purple vein throbbed in his temple.

"Your Majesty!" I cried, hurrying to cover my silken shift with a velvet robe. "What is it?"

"Campeggio has adjourned the tribunal without making a decision, and Pope Clement has called the case back to Rome!" he thundered. "Wolsey has failed me after all."

*King Henry will lose his case,* I thought, my legs growing so weak they could scarcely support me. *Perhaps he has already lost it.*

"The pope thinks that he is mightier than the king of England!" he roared. "But he is wrong!

*Wrong!* I bow to no man, least of all to the pope!" King Henry grasped me roughly by the shoulders. "By Saint George, I will not stand for it, Anne! I will break my ties with Rome. I will seize the power and the responsibility that has been mine all along: I will become head of the Church in England, and I will be the one who decides the rules!"

Before I could reply to this stunning announcement, the king stamped out of my apartments as abruptly as he had come in, slamming the door so hard that the window glass rattled.

A FEW DAYS AFTER this royal outburst, the king proved his determination. He invited me to accompany him on summer progress. I would ride in the queen's place! In recognition of my new role in the king's public life, he sent me an elegant traveling costume, as well as a new saddle, a jeweled harness, and trappings for my palfrey in black velvet fringed with silk and gold. I rejoiced at this turn in my life.

How magnificent King Henry looked on the day we left! He sat tall astride his great stallion, the morning sun sparkling on the jewels stitched to his doublet. How much I loved him! And it was clear that the king's love for me was increasing day by day. He couldn't bear to be away from me.

Yet I couldn't stop worrying. My future was far from secure. King Henry had said no more about his determination to be the one to decide the rules, and I was surrounded on all sides by people who wished me ill, chief among them Cardinal Wolsey. The uncertainty of my position gnawed at me.

The days passed pleasantly despite my worries, until we arrived at Grafton, one of the royal hunting lodges. There I learned that our guests would include the hateful Wolsey.

I could not forget that Wolsey had robbed me of my first love, Hal Percy. If the king had not yet resolved to rid himself of this incompetent chancellor, then I would convince him of what he must do and strengthen his will to do it. I was just as stubborn as Catherine and just as determined to have King Henry as my husband.

The king made it known that he wished to have private conversations with his adviser of many years, and I was not included. But I needed to learn how the king would deal with the man who had failed him. After the two had shut themselves in the king's chambers, I found a bench beneath an open window. From there I easily overheard Cardinal Wolsey's contemptuous words: "Must you persist in this folly, my lord? Once you have attained the annulment, it will be a simple matter to find you a royal bride more suitable than the lady Anne."

I gasped. How dare he! I waited to hear the king's response, his ringing praise of me, but King Henry said only, "The lady Anne will be a fit wife for me." That was all! The king, who claimed he loved me, had only *that* to say to the cardinal? I was hurt, and I was furious.

The talk then shifted to other matters in which I had no interest. As I moved away from the window, trembling with rage, I vowed, *If my future husband will not fight for me, then I must fight for myself.*

THAT SAME DAY I arranged a dinner for King Henry in my own chambers (I had brought with me several of my finest tapestries, my most luxurious cushions, my best bed-curtains and coverlets to make the rude hunting lodges more to my liking). Wolsey was not invited.

As we dined, I said carefully, "The cardinal has managed your Great Matter quite poorly, has he not, my lord?" (This was how the king referred to his efforts to rid himself of the old queen.)

"Yes, yes, sweetheart, you are right," he muttered.

I pressed harder. "In truth, his miserable efforts amount to a betrayal of yourself, do they not, my lord?"

The king glanced at me. "Betrayal? Perhaps."

"Perhaps, then, sir, it would be well to find a new chancellor. One who can bring about a happy end to it."

"That is my decision, Lady Anne!" he said sharply. Recognizing his rising anger, I retreated from the subject.

Determined to keep the king apart from his chancellor until I could find a way to persuade King Henry to get rid of him, I devised a plan. The next day I suggested a ride to a new deer park "so that I may try out my hunting bow." Then I arranged to end the hunt with a feast, and after we were done eating and drinking, I called for Nell to bring my harp, that I might entertain the king with a song, or two or three. Thus I contrived to fill the time so that when we returned to our lodgings at day's end the cardinal had departed.

I was not the only one who hated Wolsey. For weeks, Wolsey's enemies filled the king's ear with complaints against this greedy butcher's son who'd used the king's favor to amass a fortune, this churchman who was known to have fathered illegitimate children. At last, the king reached his own conclusions. Late in October, in a noisy scene in his privy chambers that I was sorry to have missed but which was reported to me by my brother, the king angrily dismissed his chancellor and ordered charges brought against him.

In an attempt to placate his master, Wolsey surrendered nearly all of his property: York Place and its priceless furnishings, including sixteen beautifully carved beds with dozens of mattresses stuffed with the finest wool; Hampton Court and its magnificent tapestries, cupboards filled with gold plate, tables laden with candelabra. My mother and I accompanied the king to admire these vast riches that now belonged to King Henry—and would soon belong to me.

"A fit wedding gift from a cardinal," I whispered

to my mother, who clucked disapproval of my mordant tongue.

MY FAMILY ROSE still higher in the ranks of the king's court and exercised ever greater influence. In December the king awarded my father two more lofty titles, earl of Ormonde and earl of Wiltshire, and ordered a grand celebration in his honor.

"You will sit by my side at the banquet, sweetheart," King Henry told me. "In the queen's place."

It would be the first time I was so honored in front of all the important nobility and their wives. I clapped my hands, as a child does, for pure delight, bringing an adoring smile to the king's lips.

I was dressed in a splendid gown of black velvet, opening upon a petticoat of white satin, with diamonds set in hearts to wear in my hair—all a gift of the king for this occasion. The banquet itself was as splendid as a wedding feast, almost as splendid as mine would surely be. And sitting in the queen's chair was just as thrilling as I had imagined, although my being there no doubt met with disapproval from some. I cared not a fig for their grumblings. I cared only that the king get on with the matter of arranging the *real* wedding. I felt I was still no closer to marriage to the king and coronation as queen, and everyone knew it. I chafed at the delays, but I could do nothing.

A few weeks later Queen Catherine returned to

court and reclaimed her accustomed place beside the king. Any joy I'd had from the banquet completely faded. I knew that the king often dined privately with her as well. My patience was beginning to wear thin as tissue, and I feared that if the wedding didn't happen soon, it might not happen at all. And I couldn't bear to think of the consequences of *that*.

Fear made me short-tempered and sharp-tongued. "I see that some fine morning you will succumb to her reasoning and cast me off," I railed at the king. "I have been waiting for a long time. By now I might have made a good marriage and had children. But, alas! Farewell to my time and my youth, wasted to no purpose at all!"

With these impassioned words, I burst into tears. The king seemed to understand that my nerves were to blame and sought to comfort me with sweet assurances.

Soon after the banquet my brother, George, now titled Viscount Rochford, was named a gentleman of the privy chamber. As I expected, George conveyed to me an endless stream of court gossip.

Some of George's news was shocking, especially regarding the king's bastard son, Henry Fitzroy, now ten years old. "He is said to be a bright young fellow. Certain of the nobility believe that the boy might be designated heir to the throne," my brother reported. "Then, for good measure, married to Princess Mary."

"Princess Mary is Fitzroy's half sister!" I exclaimed. "Certainly the pope would never permit such a union!" *But what if it's true?* I thought; *what if the king is persuaded by such an appalling suggestion?*

"I have another piece of information," George said. "This has to do with the king's sister, Mary Brandon. You insulted her, you know, at the banquet. She believes that she should have taken precedence over you and entered the hall before you."

"What nonsense! Does she still fancy herself a queen?"

"She does. And she is also the duchess of Suffolk. In either case she outranks you, dear sister, and she resents the position the king has given you. She has persuaded her husband to oppose your marriage to King Henry."

"Charles Brandon would not do that. He is the king's friend."

"True enough. But Brandon has been whispering in Henry's ear that you are not a woman of the highest reputation. That you were once betrothed to Hal Percy and later in love with Thomas Wyatt, and that you gave yourself to both these men."

"How dare Brandon say such a thing!" I exploded. "He has no knowledge of either matter. He says this simply to avenge his wife for some pretended slight!"

Nell returned with the tankards of ale I had sent her to fetch but stopped short at the sound of my angry voice. "Put them down and be gone!" I snapped. Nell did so, but not without a reproachful look.

Immediately I wished I could call my words back. I sincerely regretted that my impatience was taking its toll upon the worthy Nell, for I believed her more loyal to me than most of the ladies of the court.

MY RELATIONS WITH HENRY grew more and more difficult. Just days before the Yuletide festivities were to begin at Greenwich, I was on my way to the king's chambers when I happened upon a servant carrying a bolt of very fine linen, of the kind the king ordered woven for his shirts. I questioned the girl and learned that she was taking the linen to the queen's apartments. "For what purpose?" I asked.

"Her Majesty is to stitch His Majesty's shirts, mistress."

I was astonished. Why was the queen still performing such an intimate service for the king? A service that should have been mine? My astonishment turned to alarm that I was losing ground in my determination to become the king's wife. My alarm gave way to anger so strong that I could scarcely draw a breath. In this state I rushed into the king's chambers.

"Sir!" I cried. "What is this that I have now discovered—that the queen is your needlewoman?"

The gentlemen surrounding the king looked at me in bewildered surprise; with a gesture he dismissed them. I gave him no opportunity for reprimand but shrieked, "How could you do this to me?"

"This has nothing to do with you," the king said

brusquely. "The queen is pleased to serve me, and the shirts turn out to my satisfaction."

"It has everything to do with your love for me—or lack of it!" I cried.

"Silence, madam!" roared the king. "I will have no more of your vituperation! Now be gone with you!"

Mutely I reverenced the king three times, the blood pounding in my ears, and ran out of the privy chamber. I knew that I had pushed him too far, but I also felt deeply humiliated. I vowed to teach the king a lesson.

I would arrange my own Yuletide festivities at York Place, once Wolsey's and now mine to use as I pleased. Let King Henry do without me! Let him sit at Greenwich Palace with his worn old wife by his side, good for nothing but sewing shirts, and contemplate settling into old age with the puny princess as his only heir!

There was a risk in such a challenge to the king, but I believed I had to take it.

Within two days all was in readiness. On the Feast of the Nativity, the Great Hall of York Place smelled sweetly of rosemary and other herbs; expensive beeswax candles burned in golden candlesticks. I wore a gown made of cloth of silver and furred with sable. A boar's head with gilded tusks and dozens of other dishes were prepared for the banquet. Minstrels entertained us with their music for hours. But the Great Hall was half empty. I had invited the king and queen, as custom required; naturally, they declined. (If the king had any reaction to my plan, he didn't let me hear of it.)

My parents were there, as were my uncle, the duke of Norfolk, and his family, of whom I was not overfond. George brought his peevish wife, Jane, and various members of her family, whom I liked even less. I also yielded to my mother's entreaties and invited my sister, whom I had not seen in more than two years. Although I provided sums regularly for my nephew, Henry, who'd been made my ward, I had had almost nothing to do with Mary and her children.

And so I was appalled when Mary arrived in a threadbare gown, her children clothed in garments long outgrown and outworn, her few servants not properly liveried. I offered Mary one of my own gowns for the banquet, but she had grown ample about the waist and bosom and nothing could be found to fit her. In the end I loaned her a robe to cover her shabby gown and petticoat. The sadness in the eyes of her children prompted me to make her a large gift of money.

"You have risen so high," my sister remarked, having thanked me as she accepted the gift. "Much higher than I did. But that means you have much farther to fall. Do not forget that, Nan."

A WEEK PASSED, and I heard nothing from King Henry. I began to fear that I had gone too far. But at the New Year the king sent me a lavish gift, a velvet sack filled with gold pieces, accompanied by many loving words. From now on, he pledged, it was Catherine who would sit alone while I would have the pleasure of the king's company.

My strategy had proved successful, but my heart was not at ease. I was still not the king's wife, and I was still not the queen. I had been at court for eight years; nearly four had passed since the king had begun to pay court to me, yet I was no closer to my dream. Every time it seemed within my grasp, Fate snatched it away. Often, as I tossed sleepless in my bed, my sister's words haunted me: *You have risen so much higher than I. . . . You have much farther to fall.*

CHAPTER 12

# The Death of an Enemy

## 1530

Time was passing. How long could I keep the love of this hot-blooded man? In my growing fear and desperation, I began to make mistakes. Perhaps my first serious error was my insistence upon having the queen's jewels.

King Henry sat at a table in his privy chamber at Greenwich, a large sheet of parchment spread out before him, a quill in his hand. He was engaged in designing a complete remaking of York Place. He didn't look up when I spoke of the jewels. "What of them?" he murmured.

I opened the door of the golden cage holding a pair of linnets, and one of the songbirds hopped upon my finger. "The jewels are the property of the crown, are they not?" The linnet cocked her bright eye as I carried her nearer to the king's table. "They do not belong to Catherine herself?"

He laid aside his pen and sprinkled sand on the wet ink. "You are right, madam," he said, gazing at his work admiringly.

"I want them," I said, my voice too shrill. "I deserve to have them."

Now the king glanced up. A look of annoyance flickered in his blue eyes. "But sweetheart," he coaxed, "you have many pretty jewels, have you not?"

"That is not the issue. Catherine has no right to those jewels. They should be worn by the woman who sits by your side, who walks by your side. In a fortnight begins the Lenten season," I reminded the king, trying to keep my voice sweetly calm. "I should like to wear the queen's jewels on the Great Vigil of Easter."

I was sure that Catherine would not surrender them willingly, but I wanted to know if the king had the courage to stand up to her. Easter was two months away.

"And so you shall, dear lady," murmured King Henry, his attention already back on his drawings. "In time, you shall have all. If you will just be patient a little longer—"

"A little longer," I said bitterly. "For how much longer will you promise 'a little longer'? Until I am dead and in my grave?"

And so it went. We argued often now, my frustration erupting in angry words. I sometimes threatened to leave him, he tried to placate me, and I grew even more distressed.

It was apparent that the king grievously missed his old friend and adviser Cardinal Wolsey. King Henry had replaced him as chancellor with Sir Thomas More, a renowned lawyer and brilliant scholar. More had already shown his untrustworthiness by not adding his signature to a letter to the pope urging the head of the church to nullify the king's marriage.

"When will you stop listening to men who are so lacking in courage?" I cried when I learned of this. "I beg you, my lord, do something! Put the pope's hat on your own head, make yourself the head of the Church in England, and do that which you know to be right!"

For a tense moment the king stared at me; I met his stare for as long as I dared. Then I dropped into a deep curtsy and withdrew, leaving him to ponder my bold words.

THE LENTEN SEASON passed, my ninth as a member of the English court. Although I knew that I must speak no more of it, I found ways to remind the king of his promise to give me the queen's jewels. He ignored my hints. Easter arrived, but not the queen's jewels, and I wept with frustration. However, I was heartened when King Henry at last banished Catherine to a dank and dismal manor house far off in Hertfordshire, hoping that her will would weaken there. I hoped that she would rot. He decreed that she be called "dowager queen," a title that acknowledged her as Prince Arthur's widow but not as the king's former wife. Lady Mary, no longer titled princess, had been sent to the royal palace, Beaulieu, and then ignored, for the most part. Mother and daughter were forbidden to visit one another or even to send letters. But I was certain that those two would manage to find a means of ignoring the king's command, and I knew that Catherine still had many supporters who would always insist that she was the queen.

Even though I now occupied the queen's place, on summer progress and at feast days celebrated at Greenwich or one of the other great palaces, I was feeling increasingly desperate. In this troubled state of mind, I invited my brother to sup with me.

"I wish to recruit some spies," I told him.

"Where, Nan?" he asked, spearing a chunk of venison with his knife. "To what end?"

"In the household of the dowager queen," I said softly. "I need to know how much support the old queen really has—who her friends are, what they may be plotting. I particularly mistrust Emperor Charles's new ambassador, a man named Chapuys."

This was the kind of assignment my brother enjoyed. "A kitchen maid to observe the comings and goings of unusual visitors," my brother said, thoughtfully counting on his fingers, "a maid of the chamber to overhear conversations, and a groom to whom the queen and her friends might entrust their secret messages. That can be arranged."

"Then please see to it," I said.

I REMAINED UNEASY about Wolsey as well. Although he was no longer chancellor and stayed far to the north in York, several days' journey from Greenwich, I would not feel safe from the cardinal's manipulations until he lay moldering in his grave. But I knew that persuading King Henry of this would not be a simple task.

Then in mid-November my father paid a rare visit to my chambers. He wore a somber expression, and I sensed that something was wrong.

"I have learned that the cardinal has been working secretly with the pope," my father informed me, "and also with Emperor Charles to go against your marriage. They have persuaded the pope to issue an edict ordering King Henry, under threat of excommunication, to leave you and to send you into banishment."

I felt as though I had been struck. "We must put a stop to this!" I cried, and sank weakly upon a bench.

"Then you must convince the king to have Wolsey arrested at once. There is no time to lose."

I rushed to the king's apartments, swept past a number of gentlemen in the presence chamber, and demanded to see the king. One of the henchmen stepped forward to stop me, but I pushed by him and boldly entered the king's privy chamber.

"The cardinal is a traitor!" I cried out in front of everyone, for I wanted them all to hear what I would say. "I have proof now, and you cannot argue against it, that Wolsey has turned against you for the last time."

"Then say it, madam," the king ordered sternly.

I repeated my father's words. As he listened, the king's blue eyes narrowed and his jaw tightened dangerously.

This time he listened to me. He bellowed for the captain of the guards. "Arrest Wolsey," he barked. "And bring him to me."

Days passed; I worried that the cardinal had fled to the Continent, perhaps to Rome, before he could be seized. Then we received word that the cardinal had fallen ill and collapsed by the roadside. I suspected a trick, but only hours later Wolsey's servant appeared, already dressed in mourning. Cardinal Wolsey was dead. Secretly I rejoiced, but I also believed that he had gotten off too easily. He should have been hanged as a traitor.

WOLSEY WAS DEAD, but Catherine lived on. Her death would have simplified matters greatly, for as a widower King Henry would have been free to marry me at once.

And there was still Lady Mary, the former princess, who by all reports had turned into a delicately beautiful young woman and—as Henry liked to remind me from time to time, whenever he thought of her—a person of remarkable brilliance.

"Her Latin is faultless," the king boasted. "She reads Greek as easily as she does English and has since early childhood. She plays with great skill upon the virginals and the lute, and her tutors speak admiringly of her quick and inquiring mind."

"How nice," I responded. *How dull,* I thought.

"I have no doubt that she would make a fine ruler one day," Henry continued. I drew in my breath, dreading to hear what he might say next. "If only she were a *man*!" he finished.

I let my breath out slowly. "But she is not, my love," I said, stroking the king's hand, toying with the massive rings that encircled each large finger. "I will provide you with sons," I reminded him. "Just as soon—"

"Yes, yes, yes!" he broke in irritably. "I know all that! You need not remind me."

Prudently I held my tongue.

Then George brought me an unwelcome piece of information, conveyed to him by the spies he had placed in Catherine's household. "You will not like to hear this, dear Nan," said my brother. "For it will gravely weaken the king's case in the Great Matter."

"Please tell me quickly," I said, my throat tightening.

"Mistress Catherine, as we must now call her, insists that she was a virgin at the time of her marriage to Henry."

"But how can that be? Was she not legally married to Arthur?"

"She was. When Catherine and Arthur were wed in November of 1501, the young prince was already ill, suffering from consumption. And when he died five months later, Catherine was still an untouched virgin, so she claims. She intends to argue that, since the marriage was unconsummated, her marriage to Henry is indeed valid."

*It is her word against his,* I thought, my heart pounding. When I found my voice, I said, "No matter what Mistress Catherine claims, the marriage has ended. King Henry will make certain of that." But in my heart, I was not so sure. Only Catherine's death would truly bring an end to it.

CHAPTER 13

# Promises and Threats

## 1531

I felt the days slipping away like water, and that increased my despondency. In summer I would turn twenty-four. Every time I glanced into the mirror, I saw plainly that the first bloom of youth had faded. There were many pretty maidens at court to catch the eye of the aging king, now nearly forty.

I feared that by the time the king was free to marry, he would think me too old to be his wife and find another, younger, woman. I would be abandoned, discarded, wanted by no one. King Henry continued to profess his love for me, but on many dark nights I lay awake tormented by doubt: *Why does he not simply declare himself the head of the Church, dissolve his marriage to Catherine, and marry me—before it's too late? Does he love me ENOUGH?*

At court I was still the center of attention. The gentlemen found me alluring, but the ladies were another matter. To my face they courted my favor, but I believed that every one of them waited for me to make a misstep. I still had no close friends but my brother, and I did not trust his wife's influence upon him. Despite Lady Rochford's simpering smiles and ingratiating words—she never failed to say flattering things about my gowns and jewels—I felt that she was capable of betraying both me and her husband.

ON MAY DAY WE PREPARED to celebrate, as usual, with feasting and dancing. I had not intended to take part in the masque, but when one of the dancers, Lady Brereton, fell ill at the last moment, I agreed to take her place. I dressed in Lady Brereton's costume with my hair hidden beneath a net of gold. A headdress of elegant feathers stitched to a velvet mask concealed my face.

"You look entirely unlike yourself, mistress," said Nell wonderingly, holding a mirror so that I could admire my disguise.

And so it proved, when I found myself in the midst of a number of gentlewomen, wives of the king's favorite courtiers. All were masked, but I recognized their voices. Unaware of the exchange with

Lady Brereton and ignorant of my presence among them, they began to gossip about me.

"It seems that the king can find no way to get rid of her," said a voice I recognized as Lady Morley's, George's mother-in-law and a close friend of the former queen. "She clings to him like a nettle."

"She knows no shame!" sneered another. "She wears her hair loose upon her shoulders, as though she were still a young virgin!"

Her friend laughed softly. "She insists upon that, does she not? But I know not a soul who believes her protests!"

I trembled as the insulting words struck home, but my limbs were incapable of moving me away.

"The signs have been clear all along."

"Signs of what, pray?"

Their voices dropped, and I strained to hear.

"That she is a witch," whispered Lady Wingfield. "The little extra finger that she goes to such lengths to disguise—*that* surely is a sign. And I have heard that the blemish on her neck, always hidden beneath a jewel, is a pap where a demon comes to suck."

"I myself believe she has put a spell on King Henry!" That voice belonged to Lady Rochford, George's wife.

My heart beat faster as I listened, and my anger mounted. Blood pounded in my temples, my mouth was dry as dust, and my hands were shaking. *How dare you speak of me like this?* I wanted to shout at them. *One day I shall be queen above all of you!*

Then, as the musicians began to play and we took our places for the masque, I allowed my disguise to drop. I asked Lady Rochford for help securing it in place. I relished the look of horror that crossed each of the faces as the ladies recalled exactly what they had said against me. I would never forgive them.

AND STILL MY TROUBLES grew more serious. Early in the autumn Henry arranged a hunting party with Brereton, Brandon, my brother, and others of his favorites. "Good sweetheart," he said, taking his leave, "I shall be gone but a fortnight, and then I shall be in your arms once again."

I was lodging at Cardinal Wolsey's splendid York Place, renovated and renamed Whitehall to erase all traces of its former owner. The king had been gone for several days when my mother and I received an invitation from my aunt, Lady Anne Shelton, and her daughter, Margaret, to sup with them at their mansion on the Thames a few miles upriver from Whitehall. I was grateful for the invitation, for when the king was absent and I was alone, my fears for my future at times grew large enough to overcome me.

My brother, hearing of our plans, rushed to warn me of danger. "Crowds of angry women have been gathering to shout their ill will toward you," George told me. "They are angry because taxes have been increased, because crop failures have brought about a threat of famine, for any number of reasons that have nothing to do with you. Yet you are being blamed. You do not have the popular support that Catherine has. They do not want the king to marry you."

"What care I, if they love me or no?" I said, although in truth I *did* care, deeply. "I have the king's love. The people will come to love me when I have provided them with their future king."

"It may take more than an heir to the throne to win them over."

"And?" My lips had begun to quiver, and my eyes filled with tears. "What have they shouted, George? Pray tell me."

"Over and over they shout, 'No Nan Bullen for us!' They are a dangerous mob, dear sister. I wish that I could accompany you to assure your safety, but the king has summoned me to join him, and I must leave at once."

"Have no fear for my safety, George," I assured him with more bravado than I felt. "We will take several guards with us and travel well disguised."

And so we did, arriving without incident at the Sheltons' mansion, where we were welcomed warmly by my aunt and my cousin, Margaret, a comely girl with lustrous auburn curls.

Our conversation was suddenly interrupted by servants who rushed in to warn us of a commotion. A crowd had gathered by the gates, they said, and threatened to break through.

"They are all women," announced one of the

cook's helpers, "and they are clamoring for *you,* Lady Anne."

"For me?" I cried, greatly alarmed.

"Yes, madam. 'Nan Bullen,' they shout and demand that you come out."

"What can we do?" I wept, now thoroughly frightened. George had been right, and I had been foolish not to heed his warnings.

"Go with Margaret," said Lady Shelton. Then she ordered her servants, "Fend them off as best you can." My cousin led us to a narrow stairway, which we climbed quickly to a chamber with a small window overlooking the main gate. The narrow streets leading to the manor house swarmed with shouting women carrying knives and broomsticks. The crowd seemed to be turning into a huge and unruly beast.

I was terrified. My mother and I had only Nell and a few attendants with us, not enough guards to protect us, and my aunt's household could not be expected to hold off such a mob for long.

A young servant of the household, a boy of perhaps eleven or twelve, rushed up the stairway, his clothing in tatters, his face scratched and bloody. "I got away from them," he told us, between gasps for breath. "Mistress, you are in terrible danger! It looks like a crowd of women, but one of the vicious hags who came after me had a beard! He was dressed in petticoats and a cap to give the appearance of a woman, but I know a man when I see one."

"But what do they want?" I sobbed.

"They call for your death, my lady," said the young fellow, bursting into unmanly tears.

"What is your name, lad?" asked Lady Shelton, who had a cool head on her shoulders.

"Edward, mistress," snuffled the boy. "Son of the hostler."

"Edward, you know how to row a boat, do you not?"

Edward nodded, wiping his nose upon his sleeve.

"Fetch your father and go down to the water gate. There you will find two or three old wherries. Bail them, if need be, and wait for us there. We will come disguised as the very women who are clamoring in the streets."

"But how will I know it is you, mistress?" asked Edward.

"I will shout 'God save the king!' No one dares argue with that."

When the boy had run off to find his father, Lady Shelton summoned those servants who had not already taken refuge with us in the upper chamber and ordered them to hand over their kirtles and petticoats, their rough woolen jerkins and leather buskins and caps. My mother and I, as well as my aunt and cousin, quickly dressed in these rude garments. We hurried down to the scullery and crept out through a back entrance, groped in darkness past the stables, and descended the damp and slippery steps leading to the water gate. Two men and a boy waited by the wooden boats.

Lady Shelton called out grimly, "God save the king!" and Edward piped, "God save the king."

The boy's father and uncle helped us to climb aboard the wherries. One by one the boats slipped out onto the dark river.

"The tide is against us, my lady," said Edward's father, who had agreed to row the boat in which I huddled with my mother and Nell and two other servants, all of us quaking with terror.

"Then go with it—anything to get away from the mob—but make for the opposite shore. When the tide turns, head downriver for Greenwich."

"Not to Whitehall?" my mother whimpered, clutching my arm.

"The mob might have gone there as well," I answered.

Never had I spent a more wretched night. A heavy mist began to fall, but we had no shelter from it, and soon our rough disguises were wet and cold. On the opposite shore of the Thames, the raving mob surged angrily around Lady Shelton's mansion, their smoking torches adding an eerie glow.

"It looks like a scene from hell," muttered Edward's father as we shivered against a stone wall slick with wet moss.

The mist became a heavy rain, and the crowd began to disperse. When the tide turned sometime after midnight, our boatman headed downriver toward Greenwich, and my aunt and cousin cautiously returned to their mansion on the opposite bank.

For the moment, at least, I was safe. I sent a message to the king, who cut short his hunting party and hurried to my side.

"By Saint George, I will punish those responsible!" the king promised, but the leaders of the mob could not be found. From then on I so feared for my safety that I would not leave the palace except under heavy guard.

*Dear God, help me,* I prayed earnestly. *I cannot bear to be so hated by those I would have love me!* But if God heard my prayers, he seemed not to soften the hearts of my enemies, and my despair deepened.

CHAPTER 14

# The Last Card

## 1532–1533

"Will the woman never accept her fate?" raged King Henry, pounding the table with his fist. A richly decorated gold cup danced on the wooden board with every angry blow.

The occasion was the New Year of 1532. The old queen had not been invited to court for Yuletide. In addition, she had been ordered to stay in her far-off manor house and forbidden to send the king any further messages. But Catherine had decided that a gift was not truly a message, and she had sent the king the gold cup.

"*She* will not accept her fate because *you* do not accept it, my lord," I reminded him. "The dowager queen still maintains a household of two hundred servants, with thirty ladies-in-waiting and as many grooms and ushers. Send back the cup and take away her servants. Only then will Mistress Catherine begin to understand that she is no longer the queen."

King Henry sighed deeply. "You are right, Anne. I will do as you suggest. This is the year that we shall wed. I promise you that, as your king and the one who loves you above all else. Now come, sweetheart. I have a special gift for you."

He led me into a chamber of the palace that I had never before entered. The chamber was empty, save for a splendidly carved bed, piled high with wool-stuffed mattresses and draped with brocade bed-curtains stitched with gold braid.

"For the next queen of England," he said, with the youthful smile that always touched my heart, and he urged me to step closer to the bed. There, spread out upon the blue silk coverlet was a magnificent crimson velvet mantle. Bands of snowy ermine trimmed the front, the neck, the hem. Only the highest-ranking nobility were permitted to wear ermine, the costliest of furs! The king lifted the mantle and arranged it around my shoulders.

Thrilled with the gifts, I embraced the king and kissed him passionately. Suddenly King Henry seized me in his arms and carried me to the bed. I struggled against him, but the king was far more powerful than I. "My lord," I cried, "I beg you! If, as you say, we shall soon be wed, then we must wait a little longer."

The king groaned and released me, nearly dropping me onto the mattresses. "You are right, Anne. Once again, you are right." He walked out of the chamber, leaving me alone on the great bed, still wrapped in the dazzling ermine-trimmed robe.

THE MONTHS FOLLOWED one upon another, and I observed another birthday. Twenty-five! To think that I had once wished to be older; I now dreaded it! Still, there was cause for my hopes to rise. The king had ordered work begun on the royal apartments in the Tower of London, where by tradition I would stay on the night before my coronation. This encouraged me to believe that we would indeed soon marry, and I would soon be queen.

We set out on a summer hunting progress. "May we now choose a date for the wedding, my lord?" I asked as we rode side by side beneath a hazy sun.

The king was in an expansive mood, as he always was when he'd left behind the cares of governing, and he smiled at me fondly. "Nothing would please me more, dear Anne," he said. "But that is not yet possible. You yourself know that I have not yet obtained the annulment."

I turned my face away and bit my tremulous lip.

"There are, however, two other dates that you must reckon upon," the king continued.

My two greyhounds bayed excitedly as they scented game nearby, and the master of the hounds released them. But I was paying no attention to the dogs and wheeled to face the king. "And what might be the occasions, my lord?" I asked.

"In October you will accompany me to Calais for a reunion with King Francis. It is to be a splendid occasion—as splendid as our Grand Rendezvous at the Field of Cloth of Gold."

"It will be my great privilege!" I exclaimed, transported back in memory to that eventful day a dozen years earlier when I'd gazed upon the great King Henry VIII, and my life forever changed.

"You will travel as my intended queen, and so you must have an appropriate title. Therefore, on the first of September, I shall make you the marquess of Pembroke." King Henry beamed, clearly enjoying the surprise he'd planned for me.

Impetuously I reached for his hand and brought it to my lips. "My lord, you do me the highest honor!" *No more simply "Lady Anne"! I would have a noble title!* "But 'marquess' is a gentleman's title, is it not?"

"As I wish it to be. Most noblewomen acquire the title of marchioness through marriage. I want you to have a title that no woman has held in her own right."

Then abruptly, lured by the yelping of the hounds, King Henry saluted me and, spurring his horse, rode off in pursuit of his quarry.

THE CEREMONY TOOK place at Windsor Castle. I had attended many such ceremonies; this would be mine alone.

My parents and brother, of course, were present for the occasion, as well as my sister, to whom I'd sent a purse of gold for several new gowns. My cousin, Margaret Shelton, more comely than ever, arrived with her mother, our escape from the howling mob a distant memory. Another cousin, young Mary Howard, was chosen to carry the crimson mantle and the gold coronet. As a dozen trumpeters blew jubilant fanfares, the king, splendidly garbed in purple trunk hose slashed with cloth of gold, read out the documents granting my title. He placed the coronet upon my head as I knelt at his feet. I was now marquess of Pembroke, my rank exceeding my father's and my brother's but not my uncle's, the duke of Norfolk.

When the long ceremony ended, we moved in procession to Saint George's Chapel for the Mass, celebrated by the theologian, Thomas Cranmer. Later, the Great Hall of Windsor was the setting for a grand banquet. I wore a gown of black satin embroidered from neck to hem with hundreds of pearls.

At the end of the day I was exhausted but exultant. The common people might jeer all they wished—as they had again just weeks earlier, spoiling a late-summer hunting party—but I slept that night content in the knowledge that I was without question the most important woman in all England and would soon take France by storm.

WITH A THOUSAND attendants to accompany us on the journey, we were ready to depart for Dover and thence by ship to Calais. All that remained was for Catherine to turn over her jewels before we sailed. Yet still the old queen resisted. Henry reminded her that the jewels were not hers, but the property of the crown. Finally, Catherine yielded and returned the jewels. Riding in my splendid litter as our retinue made its way to Dover Castle, I wore them for all to see.

The royal entourage stretched for over a mile, but my personal retinue was small—much too small. Many of the ladies of the English court, among them the king's sister, had disdained the invitation to accompany me. I'd heard that the duchess's husband, Charles Brandon, had protested to the king about my part in the meeting with François. My brother's wife, Lady Rochford, had agreed to come for George's sake. If I had learned a single thing during my years as King Henry's sweetheart and intended wife, it was that only one opinion truly mattered—the king's. Still, their sniping wounded me.

One who did willingly accompany me, even riding with me in my litter, was my sister. I believed that Mary would be loyal to me, despite her occasional bouts of jealousy, and I thought she'd enjoy a reunion with her former lover, François.

"Will you be married in Calais, then?" Mary asked as the litter jolted along the muddy road. "I have heard such a rumor."

"No such plans have been made," I replied.

"Yet you travel like a queen," Mary said, "and live like a wife." She glanced at me and then looked away.

"Neither queen nor wife," I said with a sigh.

"Not like a wife?" Mary suppressed a laugh.

"I am still chaste," I said primly.

"You, Nan? Chaste?" This time Mary laughed aloud.

My temper flared. "You doubt me? I am still a virgin."

"King Henry has pursued you for six years, and you have not yet yielded your virtue? Nan, there is no one in all of Christendom who believes that!"

I began to utter a retort and then thought better of it. *Why bother to argue? I'll never convince her.*

Moodily I stared out at the long line of carts and horses plodding toward Dover. Mary reached over and laced her fingers through mine. "I have known Henry for a long time," she said. "And I can tell you what I am certain will spur him to action: if you were to conceive his son..." She squeezed my hand. "This may be your last card, Nan. Dare to play it."

*Perhaps she is right,* I thought. *Suppose I were now to conceive a child—a son! But should I risk it?* Hour after hour, day after day, I pondered the question: *Should I? Do I dare?*

ON THE ELEVENTH OF OCTOBER we set sail for Calais, a coastal town long held by the English but surrounded by France. Standing on the deck with the wind in my hair, I recalled the journey I'd made nineteen years earlier across this same water. It had been a dreadful, stormy trip, and I was a frightened little girl determined not to show her fear. Today the sky was blue, a stiff breeze filled the white sails of the *Swallow*, and the mighty king of England stood by my side. It was a relief to be leaving behind my enemies in England and sailing toward what I anticipated would be a generous welcome from the French. I felt myself at ease.

The king stepped behind me and held me fast against him so that I could feel the beating of his heart. For six years I had waited for the king to resolve his Great Matter and to make me his wife. For six years the situation had dragged on unresolved. If anything was going to change, then I must be the one to change it. If I begot a child, Henry would surely take the final step and marry me, regardless of the pope's ruling. I thought again of Mary's words: *This may be your last card. Dare to play it.*

Closing my eyes, I made my decision. I moved the king's hand to cover my breast.

That night in Calais, I welcomed King Henry into my bed for the first time.

FOR DAYS I WAITED restlessly in our lodgings while Henry met with François, first in Boulogne and then in Calais, where Henry ordered three thousand guns fired in honor of the French king.

I waited for Henry's return, and I waited for the invitations I expected from Queen Eleanor, the wife of François, and from the ladies of the French court, who were expected to entertain me. But no invitations came. There was no extravagant welcome for me, King Henry's intended bride. Nothing! I was spurned first by the queen and then by her ladies. There was not a single formal occasion at which I could make an impression with my fine wardrobe of new gowns and the royal jewels. And my sister was a witness to my humiliation.

"How can they do this to me?" I cried bitterly. "Surely the next queen of England does not deserve such rude treatment!"

Mary tried her best to comfort me. "Their behavior has nothing to do with you personally, Nan. To them you are merely a marchioness—and you will not be accorded the respect due a queen until you *are* one. Now come, let us gamble a little at cards to pass the time, until Henry comes back to you. And when he does come, do try to hide your hurt and resentment. It will only upset him."

I took what comfort I could from Mary's reasoning, but we both knew that Queen Eleanor was Catherine's niece—a fact that surely played a part in her rudeness.

And so, with little to do, I spent hours playing cards with my sister. Henry often paid my gambling debts. Now he would have to pay for both of us as we each won and lost small fortunes. And again I took Mary's advice and swallowed my wounded pride.

TOWARD THE END of our stay, Henry arranged a banquet in a hall hung with cloth of gold and gilded wreaths decorated with precious stones. Candles gleamed in twenty silver candelabra, and Henry, with my guidance, had ordered 170 dishes to be presented, half of them French and half English. I planned a masque at which I would make a grand entrance with seven ladies, all costumed in gold tissue and disguised with velvet masks. Each of us chose one of the Frenchmen as a partner; I made it a point to choose François. When the dancing had ended, the French king kissed my hand and paid me many flattering compliments.

Then he drew me aside, to speak with me in private. "Mademoiselle Anne," he said gravely, "you know that for several reasons I, as king of France, cannot approve of your proposed marriage to King Henry. The reasons, you understand, are not personal but diplomatic."

I nodded, not thinking it necessary to inform François that I had no need of his approval.

"Still," François continued, "as a personal matter, it pleases me to make you this small gift." He produced a pouch of embroidered silk and emptied the contents into my hand. A diamond as big as a walnut glittered in my palm. I guessed that Queen Eleanor knew nothing of this magnificent gift. My heart lifted.

I closed my fingers around the gem and held it to my breast. "I shall cherish it always, as I cherish your friendship," I said, and allowed François to escort me back to the gold-draped hall. King Henry rose to welcome me with a kiss, embracing me in front of everyone. Apparently he no longer cared what anyone thought.

The weather turned foul as we prepared to leave Calais, and for days it was impossible to set sail. It was mid-November when the king ordered his bed and trunks put aboard the *Swallow,* and we sailed for England. A Te Deum was sung at Saint Paul's Cathedral in thanksgiving for the king's safe return, but for once Henry was in no rush to be back at court. His love for me had blossomed anew, and he wanted my company and no other's. I returned his love in full measure.

The weeks passed happily for us both. Soon I observed certain telltale signs in my body. I prayed fervently that I was not mistaken. By Yuletide I was positive, but still I kept the secret to myself for a few days more. Then, at the New Year of 1533, my gift to the king was the greatest I could imagine: I knelt at his feet and whispered, "My lord and my love, I am carrying your child within my womb."

The king bowed his head and wept for joy.

Henry's gift to me a few days later were these

thrilling words: "I have arranged all, dearest Anne. Before the month is over, we shall be married. But it must be in secret."

ON THE COLD NIGHT of the twenty-fifth of January, the wind howled and moaned around the walls of Whitehall, rattling the windows of my chamber. Gowned in black silk and wrapped in the ermine-trimmed crimson mantle, I waited and paced fretfully.

Only loyal Nell waited with me. In another chamber of the palace my mother and father also waited, as did my brother. We had agreed that my sister-in-law, Jane, who was notoriously loose-tongued, would know nothing of this, nor would my sister, Mary.

This was hardly the kind of wedding I had dreamed of for so long, but secrecy was necessary if we were to outmaneuver the pope. Our friend, Thomas Cranmer, was soon to be named archbishop of Canterbury by Pope Clement. As archbishop, Cranmer would have the power to declare Henry's marriage to Catherine invalid. But if the pope learned first of this secret ceremony, he would surely cancel Cranmer's appointment, Henry's marriage to Catherine would stand, and the child I carried would be born illegitimate. Another bastard.

The door swung open, startling me even though I'd expected it. There stood King Henry, accompanied only by Will Brereton and a single manservant carrying a torch. The king leaned on a golden walking stick. He looked weary.

"Come," said the king, reaching for my hand.

Wordlessly the king lead me through the dark passageways, lit only by the smoking torch. Along the way, Brereton paused at a door and knocked. My parents and brother emerged and joined our silent procession.

Climbing a narrow twisting stairway, we arrived in a chamber above the Holbein Gate. Tapestries had been hung over the windows; Will Brereton and George set about lighting the candles in two large gold candelabra on a long table. From the shadows stepped a man garbed in priest's vestments; he was a stranger to me.

"I trust you have the pope's license?" the priest asked King Henry.

"Do you think I would proceed if I did not?" the king demanded haughtily. "I did not think it necessary to show it, and there is not time now to return for it. Let us proceed."

It was only a half-truth; the license the king had from Pope Clement would become valid only when the previous marriage was annulled. That had not yet happened. We were taking a great risk.

The priest looked to me for confirmation. "It is not for you to question the king," I said.

"Begin the ceremony," the king gruffly ordered the priest and again seized my hand.

Once we had exchanged our vows and the priest had pronounced the blessing, the candles were quickly extinguished, and we stole back to our separate apartments as silently as we had come. We wore no rings and agreed to tell no one what we had done. We parted without even a kiss. In this manner I became the wife of King Henry VIII.

At first it didn't seem real. As the night wore on and dawn spread slowly across the sky, I lay in my cold bed with Nell asleep by my side and marveled at what had happened: I had gambled, and I had won. I was married to the king of England and pregnant with his child. My coronation as queen of England in a few months would be followed in due course by the birth of the king's son, a future king. I had done it! I had done it all! A part of me wanted to fling open the windows and shout the glorious news for all the kingdom—no, all the *world*—to hear: *I am the queen!*

But I did no such thing, for a worm of doubt still burrowed deep in my heart and gnawed at my happiness. I reached over and shook Nell awake. "What is it, mistress?" she asked sleepily.

"There is still much that can go wrong, Nell," I whispered urgently. "I have the king's love. But can I win the people's love as well? I carry the king's child in my womb. But is it the son he wants and needs? Tell me what you think!"

"I know not the answers, mistress," she murmured drowsily. "Only God knows. You must have faith."

"I cannot rest easy until I have achieved all!" I said, but Nell was already drifting off again, and I was alone.

CHAPTER 15

# "The Most Happy"

## 1533

The secret of my pregnancy proved difficult to keep, in part due to Henry himself. His enthusiasm caused him to drop broad hints to his courtiers, calling attention to my swelling bosom and belly even before my condition might have become evident. Soon everyone was speculating.

"Cranmer has been consecrated archbishop of Canterbury, so the pope is no longer a threat," I reminded Henry. "My lord, you must make public that I am now the queen."

"In good time, sweetheart," he said, "in good time." And I had to be content with that.

Then Henry dispatched the dukes of Norfolk and of Suffolk (my uncle and Henry's brother-in-law,

Charles Brandon) to call upon Catherine in her remote manor house, informing her that King Henry was no longer her husband and she was no longer queen. I was present when the men returned with Catherine's reply.

"I have no choice but to disobey my sage and holy husband," she'd said. "I am still the queen. There is no other." Then, the dukes reported, she'd shown them her servants' new livery, embroidered with her initial entwined with the king's.

My hatred of the old queen grew fiercer. Why would she not let go? "She does it for Lady Mary's sake," said the duchess of Norfolk, an explanation that infuriated me.

"Then I shall make a servant of Lady Mary," I threatened, adding, "and I shall marry her to some varlet."

I would have done so, had the king not always taken the part of his daughter. I understood well that Mary was a danger to my position, as well as to that of the child I carried, and would remain a danger for as long as she lived and could inherit the throne. Only now do I understand that my treatment of Mary was another serious error.

TOWARD THE END OF LENT, Henry drew me onto his knee and said, "The time is right. Beginning on Easter Eve, you shall be addressed as 'Queen Anne.'"

Joyfully, I embraced the king, thanked him with

kisses, and immediately began to plan my appearance at the festal Mass in the chapel royal.

On the Saturday night that ended Passiontide, trumpets blew a royal fanfare, and I made my entrance accompanied by a suite of sixty ladies who had suddenly declared themselves to be my supporters. I was garbed in a white gown with sleeves lined in crimson satin and a new mantle of cloth of gold. All the important nobles were present. The new archbishop, Thomas Cranmer, called for the worshipers to pray for "beloved Queen Anne," and as I made my way down the aisle of the chapel, everyone bowed low. Whether they liked it or not, I was their queen.

Whitsunday, the seventh Sunday after Easter, was chosen as my coronation day. Seven weeks was not much time to prepare for an event of such importance. But there was good reason for haste; our child was expected in September, and for the infant's sake as well as for mine, we could delay the arduous ceremonies no longer.

Yet there was so much to do: My coronation gown had to be fashioned to conceal my growing belly, my golden throne to be built and the cloth of estate designed to hang above it, my crown to be created by the royal goldsmiths and jewelers. Jousts had to be arranged, banquets planned, guests invited. All of this involved great expense, but many people balked at turning over the taxes needed to pay for such a large celebration; the king had to order them to do so. Resentment swelled among our subjects. I was determined to ignore the complainers and their complaints—another error.

I devised an emblem, a crowned white falcon on a bed of red and white roses, and chose a motto to be embroidered on my blue and purple livery: *La Plus Heureuse*—"The Most Happy."

But the motto was a lie. I was far from happy. Once my marriage was made public, I was no longer simply Lady Anne, no longer the marchioness, and I could no longer be ignored. I was now the queen, the highest-ranking woman in the land. No one, save the king, was my equal. Every knee had to bend to me; everyone had to look up to me. At last I had achieved what I'd always wanted, but I was more alone and solitary than ever.

I could no longer even enjoy the attentions of the gentlemen of the court. There were scarcely any women with whom I might share a walk in the garden or a lighthearted conversation over a goblet of ale. Had it not been for the simple kindnesses of dear Nell, my maidservant, I would not have had the pleasure of any female discourse at all. So, although I had reached my goal of becoming queen, I recognized that I was losing the last of my support.

Even my family seemed to resent my new position. My father, required by royal custom to kneel in my presence, scarcely bothered to conceal his vexation. "Such ambition in a woman is unseemly," said he, the most ambitious of men! My mother frowned and looked uncomfortable in my presence. My sister behaved correctly, kneeling at my feet as I had long ago told her she would do, but I could sense her jealousy seething beneath the surface: *I deserved this more than you.*

Only George was unfailingly good-humored, immediately dropping to one knee whenever he visited my chambers, and my response to him was cheerful: I laughed, raised him up, and embraced him. I neither expected nor received any warmth from Lady Rochford.

Many in the kingdom remained stubbornly loyal to the old queen and to the former princess. At first, their feelings scarcely troubled me. Once I had provided them with the heir to the throne that they had longed for since the coronation of their young king, Henry VIII, nearly twenty-five years before, I would be welcomed into the hearts of even my most reluctant subjects.

Still, it was painful to learn that I was called the Great Whore by some of my enemies, a witch by others. Their slanders became louder and more vicious as coronation day drew closer.

"You must demand that these lies stop," I insisted, weeping angry tears. Henry sent out orders forbidding anyone to speak ill of me and offered rewards to those who would come forward to denounce anyone who did. He commanded the clergy to pray for me by name, but many persisted in praying instead for Queen Catherine and Princess Mary. Nothing helped. The people hated me, and their ill will ate steadily at my soul.

JUST DAYS BEFORE my coronation, Archbishop Cranmer finally declared Henry's marriage to Catherine null. An official decree declared Mary illegitimate and therefore unfit to inherit the throne. The last obstacle was gone. I was dizzy with relief.

Accompanied by my ladies of the court, I rode upriver from Greenwich to the Tower of London. The royal barge, painted in my colors of blue and purple and bearing my falcon emblem, was escorted by hundreds of small boats decorated with flowers and silk streamers and carrying musicians playing merry tunes. Cannons boomed a deafening welcome as I stepped ashore at Tower Wharf. Henry waited in my newly prepared chambers in the Tower. By tradition, the king would observe all of the coronation ceremonies in secret. I knew he hated that tradition—it was his nature to be at the center of everything.

Henry was occupied that night with a ceremony creating eighteen new Knights of the Bath, many of them my relatives. I tried to sleep, but in my sixth month the babe who leaped in my womb was as strong and restless as his father, and the calming potion that Nell brought me was of no help. As I lay awake in the sumptuous bed, I experienced again that fleeting shadow of doubt: *What if the babe is not a son, but a daughter?* I tried to drive off the qualm—

*Nonsense! Of course it is a son!*—but the doubt would not leave me.

FOR YEARS I'D AWAITED this day. Under a perfect blue sky I climbed into my litter, furbished in white satin and cloth of gold; the two palfreys that bore the litter were trapped in white damask. I had chosen a gown of cloth of silver, the better to show off my dark hair, which fell almost to my waist, and my many jewels. The ladies who rode behind me wore crimson velvet. A canopy of cloth of gold held above me by my gentlemen ushers glinted in the sunshine.

Most of Henry's courtiers joined the procession in a show of support for their monarch and his wife, but some did not—such as Thomas More, successor to Wolsey. More, who'd resigned his post as chancellor a year earlier, never tried to hide his disapproval of our marriage. Most of the planning for the coronation had rested in the hands of Thomas Cromwell, once Wolsey's assistant, who had craftily worked his way into the inner circle of the king's most trusted advisers.

At last, the procession moved forward.

It was my intention to wave and smile as I passed the crowds gathered along the way. But there were no cheers, no caps tossed into the air as my litter lurched through the narrow, rutted streets. The common people stared sullenly, like stupid sheep. Mostly there was silence.

Early that morning I had been visited by my

chaplain, who advised me to pray to be a wise and good ruler, and I'd snapped at him, "Better to pray that my subjects show wisdom and goodness!" I couldn't forget the mob that would have killed me on the night I managed to flee across the river. And I couldn't ignore the painful insults shouted whenever I went abroad with the king: "No Nan Bullen for us! No Nan Bullen!"

"Your Majesty, you must turn the other cheek," counseled the chaplain, "as the good Christian lady that you are. Find it in your heart to forgive those who sin against you."

"Forgive them? Impossible!" I cried. "They are unworthy of forgiveness!"

"We are, all of us, unworthy of forgiveness, dear lady, and yet God forgives us."

"Then let God forgive them, for I shall not." I did not tell the priest that I was too deeply hurt to forgive them so easily.

ON THE FIRST DAY of June, *anno domini* 1533, in Westminster Abbey I was crowned Queen Anne of England. What I thought would be the most triumphant day of my life turned out to be a day of misery.

I wore robes of purple velvet, furred with ermine; my long train was carried by my grandmother, dowager duchess of Norfolk. Dozens of churchmen and hundreds of noblemen and their wives participated in the ritual that lasted all morning. By the end of the solemn High Mass, during which I prostrated myself before the altar and was anointed by Archbishop Cranmer, I was weary to the bone. But I still had to endure the slow procession through the sullen crowds. My head throbbed, my back ached from the jolting of the litter. I closed my eyes and tried to ignore my discomfort.

As Nell bathed my face with scented water and laced me into another gown, sparkling with tiny jewels, I groaned, "With all my heart I wish that this, the greatest day of my life, at an end!" But long hours yet remained.

At Westminster Hall I was seated on the king's marble chair at a long table on a dais above the other guests. Hidden behind a screen in a gallery above me, the king dined in the company of important foreign ambassadors. Several ladies, including my sister, stood by me; others crouched under the table, ready to do my bidding as time crept by. Everything had been done to improve my comfort, including the installation of a chamber pot within the king's chair so that I could relieve myself discreetly, as was frequently necessary, now that my condition was well advanced.

Two noblemen on horseback escorted the Knights of the Bath, who paraded into the hall, carrying twenty-eight dishes for the first course, which were presented first to me. Two more courses followed, each one followed by a subtlety, a marvelous construction of sugar. Guests seated at the lower tables were offered fewer dishes, but by all accounts everyone was satisfied with the richness of the banquet. Well they should have been, for it had cost the king—and the kingdom—a large fortune.

At last it was over! The official ceremonies ended, but the next day, Monday, was the event the king himself lived for: jousting in my honor in the new tiltyards at Whitehall, followed by more feasting and dancing. Although the common people had jeered at me, the nobility had to pay me great honor, and I was gratified—if not "the most happy."

NOW I HAD ONLY to await the birth of the prince in order to achieve all that I set out to do. My mood improved.

The summer passed pleasantly, save for the death of Henry's sister, Mary. She had suffered from an illness that prevented her attendance at my coronation, but I was sure she would have found an excuse in any case. The duchess had been insulted when I was allowed to walk ahead of her. Now she would have no further complaints! After the funeral we observed a brief period of mourning, but any sadness I might have felt was assuaged by the arrival of my coronation gift from the king of France. François had sent me a magnificent litter with three beautifully trained mules to carry it.

In July my husband and I traveled by barge upriver to Windsor Castle. Out of concern for me,

Henry had given up his customary summer progress. "I can as well hunt in the forests at Windsor," he assured me. "And you can entertain guests as you wish."

And entertain I did. There were banquets nearly every afternoon, music and dancing in the evenings, and flirtations at every hour. Watching my pretty young maids of honor practice their artful wiles upon the men of the court, I remembered when I had been such a maid and the young King Henry's roving eye had fallen upon me, as it had often fallen upon other damsels of Catherine's court.

Somewhere, I thought, among the primped and powdered maids who swirled about me, was one—perhaps more than one—who would surely set out to capture the king's fancy, if only for a night or a fortnight. I watched them, trying to guess who she might be, and seethed as my choice fell upon first one, then another.

Jealousy and the tiresome waiting drove me to fits of despair and bursts of temper that ended in tears. Yet, despite harsh words that I often regretted but could not stop, Henry responded with tenderness. Although I frequently felt unwell, our time together during those weeks was the best it had ever been. Henry was so much in love with me that I could have asked him for the moon and stars, and he would have gathered them for me.

Henry spent hours planning for the arrival of his

son and heir. He drew up announcements of the birth, with the name and the date to be filled in when the child was born. He was still deciding upon a name: It would be either Henry or Edward.

"There will be jousts in the prince's honor," Henry said. "And great feasts. All the nobility of the realm will be invited, and I expect King Francis and the ruling monarchs of Europe to come. Even Emperor Charles cannot very well ignore this, for the marriage is valid and there is no question of the boy's legitimacy."

THE TIME DREW NEAR for my confinement. On the twenty-first of August, Henry and I left Windsor for Greenwich. A few days later I took formal leave of the court and retired to my chambers, where I would await the birth surrounded by my ladies-in-waiting.

I felt heavy and ungainly. My ankles were swollen. What had become of the slender body with the narrow waist and the small, firm breasts of which I had been so proud? The body once so much desired by the king had been taken over by this rollicking infant.

By custom, the windows of the suite set aside for the birth were covered with tapestries, and we spent the sultry days in a gloomy, nearly suffocating world. The bed that Henry had given to Catherine at the time of Mary's birth was moved into the innermost chamber, where I would labor and be delivered.

Nearby, two cradles stood ready for the infant. Except for my husband and the physicians, no men were permitted beyond the curtain hung in the presence chamber to preserve my privacy. I would not leave these chambers until several weeks after the birth.

Like my withdrawal from masculine company, the presence of Lady Mary was also a matter of tradition. "Tradition be hanged!" I shouted when I learned that my stepdaughter had been summoned to witness the birth of the babe who would replace her as heir to her father's throne.

It was Nell's thankless task to bring me word of her arrival. "Where shall we accommodate the lady Mary, madam?" she asked.

I thought for a moment. "In the part of the palace reserved for merchants and travelers," I said.

Nell stared at me in disbelief. "But, Your Majesty...," she began.

"Lady Mary has no royal title, no standing at all!" I cried. "Let her stay where others of her kind are allowed to rest." Then I added, "Tell her I expect her to pay her respects to me at once."

The king's beloved pearl of the world appeared much later, dressed in a worn kirtle. She was now seventeen, and despite her poor dress, rather pretty. I'd had no conversation with her in more than six years, since her betrothal to François, although I'd often seen her at court before the king had sent her away. Now we glowered at each other. I loathed her on sight, and I knew from her eyes that she loathed me as well.

"Have you no manners?" I cried. "Then we shall have to teach you some! Kneel!"

Mary sank to her knees, and I explained what her life would be like from now on. "You will serve the infant prince. It will be your privilege to change his napkins whenever they are wet or soiled. That will teach you some humility."

"And if it is a daughter, madam?" she asked insolently.

I was infuriated. Every expert her father and I consulted had assured us that the signs were all in agreement: The child in my belly was male. With scarcely a thought except to rid myself of my wretched stepdaughter, I snatched up a silver goblet and flung it at her, followed by a golden pomander and anything else I could seize. Lady Mary fled.

But I would not let her go so easily. I had to break her will, to force her to acknowledge me as queen. And so every day thereafter I summoned Lady Mary from what I hoped were her uncomfortable quarters to stand or kneel by me until I thought of some demeaning chore for her to perform. Eventually I hit upon a fine idea: I ordered her to help me to my chamber pot. Thinking of ways to humiliate the girl with her father's red-gold hair and his blue eyes was simply a way of passing the time as the days moved slowly, slowly toward the hour of the birth of my child, England's future king. But Mary neither broke nor bent.

ON A SATURDAY MORNING in early September my pains began. I remember little of the hours that followed, save that the labor was long and arduous. In the beginning I was jubilant—at last the day had come! But as the hours passed, I became weary and at last wished only that it be finished. With each pain my ladies tried to encourage me, "The king's son is coming!" But in time even that failed to hearten me.

At last, before dawn on the morning of the seventh day of September, *anno Domini* 1533, the heir to the throne of England slid into the world. Moments later I heard the newborn's lusty cries. *I have done it! I have done it!*

But then I realized that I'd heard no sound from those around me. Only minutes earlier the room had been filled with midwives and physicians; my aunt, Lady Shelton; even the wretched lady Mary, had stood wide-eyed at the foot of my bed! Now they all seemed to have melted away.

I gripped the sleeve of the head physician, who hovered at my side. "Why are you silent?" I gasped. "Why are there no cheers for the future king?"

"Madam," he said gravely. "The infant is a girl. You have given the king a new princess. A fine healthy daughter."

"No! No!" I shrieked, thinking at once of Henry

and how he would respond to this awful disappointment. I had failed! Failed! "No, it cannot be!"

My wails and sobs went on and on, seeming to come from someone else. I had not done it after all, and I feared that the king would not, could not, forgive me this fault.

*CHAPTER 16*

# Suspicions and Accusations

## *1533–1536*

The king glanced at the infant sleeping in her cradle. Then he came to stand at the side of the great bed, where I lay gazing up at him, exhausted and fearful. "So you have borne a daughter," he said in a voice laden with sadness and bitter disappointment.

"Yes, my lord," I whispered.

Suddenly his face contorted with anger. "They lied to me!" he exclaimed. "The soothsayers, the astrologers, the physicians—every one of them swore to me that it would be a male child!"

I said nothing, grateful that his displeasure was not directed against me.

"Lying to the monarch is treason, and they know

it well!" he raged, pacing about the birth chamber. "I shall have them hanged for their false words!" His ringing voice woke the infant, who commenced howling lustily, until one of the rockers tiptoed in and lifted her from her cradle to soothe her.

He stared down at me as though I had deliberately contrived to dash his hopes—as though his hopes were not my own as well. "My lord," I said, tears coursing down my face and onto my pillow, "surely I have done nothing to deserve this unhappy fate! I have prayed daily for many months, with all my heart, to give you a son..."

"Never mind," he interrupted brusquely. "You are not to blame." But there was no warmth, no forgiveness, in his voice. And he left me to deal alone with my failure and my fear.

WITHIN HOURS HERALDS were sent forth to proclaim the birth of the king's child. Three days later she was carried in a purple velvet robe to the church of the Observant Friars, where she was christened at the great silver baptismal font by Archbishop Cranmer and named Elizabeth, for Henry's mother who'd died when he was a boy.

By tradition, Henry and I did not attend the ceremony, but hundreds of others were present. Elizabeth's half sister, Lady Mary, was forced to listen as the infant was proclaimed Princess of Wales, Mary's former title. How that must have galled her!

Most of the grand celebrations were canceled. The birth of a princess did not warrant the jousting that a prince deserved. Still, there were fireworks and bonfires and public fountains spouting wine, the kind of revelry expected by the king's subjects at the birth of a royal child.

Although he had declared me blameless, it was obvious that the king still held me responsible. I had not yet risen from my bed when I resumed my petitions to Almighty God, praying fervently that I would again conceive as soon as I was able. *Hear my prayer, O Lord, I beg you, and grant me a son!* If God truly turned his back on me, I stood to lose all I had achieved.

Witnessing my distress, my aunt, Lady Shelton, tried to comfort me. "King Henry has no intention of abandoning you. 'I love her, more than ever'—those were his words," my aunt insisted. Although I wished to believe her, I could not.

But Lady Shelton did not tell me that the king had already begun an affair, although it was rumored to be with her own daughter, my cousin, Margaret! This I heard from Lady Rochford, who plainly enjoyed being the bearer of these tidings. I silently cursed them all—my aunt, my cousin, my sister-in-law, my faithless husband. I had to find a way to win him back.

EARLY IN DECEMBER, Elizabeth, Princess of Wales, bundled in furs in a splendid litter, was carried in a great procession to Hatfield Palace. Hatfield, a journey of several hours north of Greenwich, would become the royal nursery under the governance of Lady Anne Shelton.

The former Princess of Wales, Mary, had long since taken herself off to her residence at Beaulieu, but I had a few surprises in store for her. I dispatched my uncle, the duke of Norfolk, to call upon her and to inform her that I had given Beaulieu as a gift to my brother and his wife and that she would now move to Hatfield to become waiting woman to the infant Princess Elizabeth. I forbade her to take her governess with her. Lady Mary would fend for herself.

Henry shared my bed once more, yet I sensed that he came to me now solely out of duty. I knew that I must conceive another child, a son, and quickly, or all would be lost. But worry and distress were taking a heavy toll, and I frequently railed at all around me. I'm ashamed to say that poor devoted Nell often received the brunt of my growing desperation.

EARLY IN THE NEW YEAR the king and his Parliament passed two important laws. The Act of Supremacy required every citizen to swear an oath of loyalty to King Henry as supreme head of the Church in England. This meant that the pope no longer had the power to declare my marriage to Henry illegal—at long last the king had carried out his threat made five years earlier. The Act of

Succession declared Henry's marriage to me valid and declared my children by him the legitimate successors to the throne.

But many still spoke slanderously of me; many more remained loyal to the old queen and to Mary. And Henry Fitzroy, now fifteen, was summoned home from France, where he'd been at court. The king didn't bother to explain why he had done this, but I feared that if I did not soon produce a male heir, Fitzroy might actually be considered the true prince.

Not long after this I traveled with my retinue to Hatfield to visit my infant daughter. The king did not accompany me. Eagerly I looked forward to seeing her. Princess Elizabeth, a comely child who already showed a marked resemblance to her father, was thriving to everyone's satisfaction—I was kept informed of her progress by weekly messages—but Lady Shelton seemed greatly vexed by the behavior of Lady Mary.

"She is insolent and impertinent," complained my aunt. "She still fancies herself a princess and refuses to answer to anyone who addresses her as 'Lady Mary.' She will not eat with Princess Elizabeth, who naturally occupies the place of honor; the lady Mary claims that place rightfully belongs to her. Whenever the princess rides in her special litter, the lady Mary refuses to walk behind her, as precedence requires. Madam, I have never witnessed such defiance, as you shall see with your own eyes!"

Lady Shelton was correct. I made no attempt to speak to Mary but gave this order to Shelton: "Show Lady Mary no kindness or understanding. Slap her whenever she exhibits such outrageous insolence, and at other times as you see fit. And remind her, whenever possible, that she is nothing but an accursed bastard."

"Perhaps I might also remind her that the king would have her beheaded if she does not yield?"

I hesitated for only a moment. "Perhaps," I agreed. Although Henry was angry at Mary for her stubbornness, he had not even hinted at such a drastic measure.

What I would not now give to call back those cruel words!

IN THE EARLY SPRING my most heartfelt prayers were answered: I conceived another child. King Henry celebrated by ordering a beautiful silver cradle ornamented with Tudor roses and set with precious gems, and once again I enjoyed Henry's favor. My confidence returned that I would present the king with a male heir and secure my future as queen.

But Lady Mary was still an irksome problem. I decided to try a new tactic: I would attempt to improve my relationship with Mary—not for Mary's sake, but for Henry's—knowing that would benefit me as well. On a springtime visit to my precious Elizabeth, I sent Mary a carefully worded note, offering to welcome her if she would but acknowledge me as queen and inviting her to sup with me. I inquired of the cooks at Hatfield what foods Lady Mary might especially enjoy, but no one seemed to know; Shelton had ordered her to eat with the servants.

And what reply to my kindness did I receive? This curt note was delivered to my chambers:

> *I know not of any other queen in England than Queen Catherine, my mother. And if it should please the king's mistress* [This was how she referred to me!] *I should be most grateful if she would interecede with my father on my behalf.*

First she insulted me, and then she begged a favor!

I departed from Hatfield without ever having laid eyes on my ungrateful stepdaughter. Riding back to Greenwich in my litter, I wished there were some way to get rid of both Mary and her mother; I knew that, for as long as they lived, they and their supporters would plot against me.

As I brooded upon this, Henry announced that he would again travel to France. He wished to secure the king's promise to come to England's aid should the emperor—that spiteful nephew of the spiteful old queen—decide to invade England on his aunt's behalf, a possibility that worried Henry. I was in no condition to make such a long and difficult journey, but I did not attempt to dissuade Henry from going. In the king's absence, I would rule as regent. And with him far away, I would be free to use my authority to rid myself of the detestable Lady Mary, once and for all. I thought of poison. Perhaps I could bribe an apothecary to prepare a potion to be given secretly, in small doses. But who would administer the potion? Perhaps my brother could again help me.

"Do not be a fool, Nan," George cautioned when I hinted at my plan. "The king will not forgive you if any harm comes to her. You risk too much for too little in return."

"I am her death and she is mine," I told George, but in the end I knew that my brother was right. Mary lived on.

THE INFANT'S BIRTH was to be in late summer. This time my husband didn't cancel his summer hunting progress to stay at my side, but went wherever he wished, whenever he wished. When he was absent, I imagined him with my cousin, auburn-haired Margaret. This conviction preyed on my mind, until I became half mad with suspicion.

"You have waited until I am utterly at your mercy to show your affections to another woman," I scolded Henry. "Why can you not rejoice in the son I am about to give you?" I cried. "Do I no longer matter to you?"

I regret my intemperate words, surely another

grievous error. In the past when we'd argued, Henry tried to calm me or simply left until I'd regained my composure. This time he did neither. He lost his temper.

"Shut your eyes and endure what you must!" he bellowed. "Remember that it is I who have raised you from nothing, and it is I who at any time can lower you to where you were."

For days we quarreled. Finally some measure of peace was restored, but I was left with the nagging fear that he had found solace from the flames of my anger in the arms of another, younger, slenderer, and more agreeable, woman.

THE FEW PEOPLE around me offered small comfort. My mother was with me at times, and yet I found no solace in her. I had my petulant sister-in-law, Jane, whose company was worse than none at all. Mary Howard, another of my cousins, had recently married Henry Fitzroy; now I feared that she would produce a child to supplant my own as the king's heir. The duchess of Norfolk made no secret of her dislike of me, and Lady Wingfield, who'd been a friend of Henry's sister, bore me great malice. Of all the ladies in my court, only Madge Lee, sister to my old admirer, Tom Wyatt, seemed to offer true friendship, but, when I most needed her, she was called away by the illness of her son.

My sister, Mary, was one of my ladies-in-waiting.

She had been widowed for a half dozen years and suffered financial difficulties. I knew that she had pawned her jewels, and sometimes she came to me for money. Our father was cold to her, as was always his way. Occasionally I invited her to spend time alone with me, and on one such visit she confided shocking news: "I am with child," she said.

"With child?" I gasped. "With *whose* child?" In panic I remembered her earlier affair with the king.

Covering her face with her hands, Mary confessed that some months previous she had secretly married one William Stafford, a man of neither wealth nor rank. "The child is his," she whispered.

I was stunned. "You are nothing but a fool!" I cried. "Not only have you married far beneath you, but you have married without royal permission! Your life is ruined, as you must surely realize."

"Love overcame reason," Mary sobbed. "I loved him as well as he did me. Knowing how little the world thinks of me, I decided to forsake all other ways to live a poor and honest life with him."

"How could you embarrass the king and me and the entire Boleyn family in this way?" I demanded.

She glared at me defiantly. "I had rather beg my bread with him than to be the greatest queen christened."

*How dare she be happy? How dare she carry a child by the man that she loves?* I could imagine that she would bear him a fine, healthy son, while I struggled hard to attain the same end. Even now I was jealous of my sister.

It was my duty to tell Henry what my sister had done. I greeted him with the news when he had returned from one hunting progress and had not yet left on another. "A disgrace!" he shouted. "She must leave court at once!"

I called Mary to my chambers for the last time and delivered the king's message with little compassion. "His Majesty and I wish never to set eyes again upon such a pitiable creature as you!"

Mary bowed her head and was gone. For a moment I wished that I could call her back to embrace her. But I did not.

THE DAYS DRIFTED by slowly. I awaited my confinement, indulging my passion for gambling at cards, always losing the money that Henry allotted me for that purpose. I sometimes played the harp. I disliked watching others dance when I could not. My ladies prattled about fashion, and I dressed in gowns with panels added to accommodate my growing belly. I became increasingly restless and short-tempered. The king paid me little attention.

Francis Bryan, one of the king's favorites, brought me the gift of a little French dog to distract me. I made much of the dog, named Purkoy, until he slipped out of an open window and fell to his death. I wept for days, not only for dear little Purkoy, but for all that was lost. The years were passing, and I would never again be young and beautiful. Nothing cheered me except the belief that in a few weeks the ordeal would end, and I would have presented the king with a son.

But what if it were not a son? What if I bore yet another daughter? I could not trust the prognostications of the soothsayers or the physicians. I plagued Nell for reassurances. "What say you, Nell?" I demanded, stroking my round belly. "A boy, surely?"

But Nell, worriedly twisting a handkerchief, would say only, "God alone knows, madam. The rest of us must wait to see what blessings he sends us."

"Another daughter is no blessing," I said shortly.

And then, while the king was away on progress, the unthinkable occurred: I awoke to find myself bathed in blood and knew at once that I had lost the child. I screamed for Nell.

In great secrecy the king was summoned. With Nell clutching my hand, we both sobbed as we awaited with dread Henry's return. His forgiveness would not be won so easily this time. But when at last he stood by my bedside, I could not stop myself from turning the blame back on him: "You left me here alone, while you were off indulging yourself in your selfish pleasures!" Knowing that he might have been with another woman fueled my anger.

I hurled cruel words at Henry; Henry hurled back his own. I accused him of selfishness; he accused me of unwarranted pride. The only thing upon which we could agree was to tell no one of this loss, to swear to secrecy the physicians and servants who had attended me, and to pretend to the world that nothing had happened. Who would dare question us?

"Let no one speak of this," I commanded Nell, "by order of Their Majesties, the king and queen."

"But, Your Majesty," she said timidly, "how can you erase the memory of everyone who saw you great with child?"

"They will forget," I said with far more confidence than I felt, "as soon as I am with child once more."

I had to accomplish this quickly, and I was thoroughly frightened that I might not succeed. I was twenty-seven, and my position as delicately balanced now as it was before my marriage. The king could easily find another woman, someone younger to give him sons; I sensed that he already had. He could find a pretext to have our marriage annulled and send me away to live out my days in penury in some moldering castle far from court, as he had the old queen. What had happened to our love? Somehow it had faded, or worn out, or simply withered away. Perhaps he had already begun the proceedings to rid himself of me.

I LEARNED HER NAME: Jane Seymour. She had come to court as one of my ladies-in-waiting, small, dainty, prim, quiet. Soon I discovered that many members of the court were befriending her, and that she had even sent kind letters to Lady Mary, working her way into Mary's affections. I was frantic with fear and apprehension, and yet I was helpless to get rid of my rival. Henry made no attempt to hide his affair, and he decreed that she should stay.

"Do you care nothing for me?" I cried, although I knew the answer. "For our future children?"

"Silence!" he roared. "You should be content with all that I have done for you. Do you think that I would raise you up again, if I had it to do over? Give you titles and lands and riches? Madam, I would not!"

His harsh words plunged me into deepest misery. I could feel my life unraveling. And yet I had to find the will and the strength to continue on. My very life depended upon it.

I began to live, not only in anger and humiliation, but in endless dread. I knew that I had to conceive another child. It was the only way left to me to save my position. If I bore him a son, he would not put me aside. If I did not, it was finished. I was ruined. But how to lure a man who was always angry with me and who was plainly in love with another? I paced my chambers and spent hours at prayer, searching for an answer.

Now it was clear to me that it was because of Catherine and Mary that I had not yet borne a son. As long as they remained alive, I would not fulfill my destiny of providing Henry—and all England—with an heir and future king. But how could I persuade Henry? It was far too dangerous to try. I would bide my time and pray that Mistress Jane had not yet fully taken my place.

I STRUGGLED TO WIN back the king's favor. I arranged a number of banquets and entertainments for him. We went on a long and leisurely progress that took us far from London. The hawking had never been better. We talked amicably, our times were merry, and we became lovers again.

Finally, in January of 1536, we received the good news I had long awaited: Catherine was dead! There was suspicion of poison, and claims by the embalmer that the dead queen's heart had been black through and through lent credence to the rumor. I was suspected by some, although it was none of my doing.

In celebration King Henry and I dressed in yellow satin. Our daughter, the princess Elizabeth, who had not yet been returned to Hatfield at the end of the Yuletide season, attended Mass with us. After we dined, Henry carried Elizabeth to the Great Hall and joined in the dancing, with his little daughter in his arms. It pleased me to see how he doted on our child whenever she was brought to visit us.

There was even more good news, the best possible: I had conceived for the third time. The birth would come in summer. I had prayed hard for this, but now

I prayed even harder: *Please, dear God, this must be a son, a healthy boy!*

But my happiness was marred when I happened upon Jane Seymour perched upon the king's knee. I ordered her away, and after she fled, the king and I stared at one another. A great silence fell between us, for there was nothing to say that had not been said many times before.

Henry was entertaining friends at a joust in celebration of Catherine's death when ill fortune overtook us yet again. On the orders of my physician, I was not present. Henry insisted upon entering the lists, as he had done to such good effect as a younger man. But he was unhorsed, and his enormous warhorse fell upon him, knocking him senseless.

My uncle, duke of Norfolk, brought me the news of the mishap when Henry had awakened. I was much distressed and moaned and wept, and it was not until I had seen with my own eyes that the king was alive that I felt somewhat easy again.

But the shock was too great. Six days later, on the twenty-ninth of January, I lost the child. Nell, her poor face stained with tears, told me that, according to the physician who attended me, the tiny life I no longer carried had been a male. I was inconsolable. I blamed Mistress Jane, and I blamed Henry.

"My lord," I cried, "can you not see that it was my too great love for you that was at fault?"

But he had few words of comfort for me. "I see

that God will not give me male children," he said ruefully, "as he will not allow you to bear them."

His jaw set hard as stone, he turned away from me. I knew at that moment that the king had closed his heart against me, and I sank into fathomless despair.

CHAPTER 17

# Last Days

## 1536

The king rode off to London to his own amusements while I was still recovering from the shock of the loss of the babe in my womb, and I was left alone, tormented with grief and worry.

I had no need to be told what everyone was saying quite openly: that my marriage to King Henry was over, that he would banish me as he had Catherine, that he would lose no time in marrying his new love, Jane Seymour. Thomas Cromwell, who now held the post of king's secretary, would arrange it all. Cromwell was the most powerful man at court, and scarcely anyone would protest what he did. What had happened to Catherine was now happening to me. But the former queen had many friends and supporters; I had none.

My brother called upon me. The usually high-spirited, good-humored George Boleyn appeared deeply troubled, his face drawn and haggard. "There are matters of which you must be aware," George confided when we were alone. "You have not much time."

"Then tell me quickly," I said, my heart hammering fiercely against my ribs.

"I have learned that Cromwell has turned over his apartments here at Greenwich to Jane's brother, Edward Seymour. The apartments have a private passage leading from the king's privy chamber, and the king often uses this passage to visit Lady Jane. Chaperones are always present. He sends her lavish gifts, which she thanks him for and then returns. She flaunts her virtue. Cromwell misses no opportunity to remind the king that she is the opposite of you in every way. The king appears enchanted."

The gravity of my situation fell heavily upon me. "What can I do?" I cried, nearly undone by my anguish. "Cromwell's influence on the king is greater than even Wolsey's was!"

"Pray that the enchantment ends, and soon."

When Henry returned from London days later, I sought again to speak to him, although it was clear that he wanted to avoid me. He gazed at me with cruel, glittering eyes as I knelt as his feet.

"It was because of the love I bear you that I lost the child," I wept, my hands lifted in pleading. "You know that I love you more than Catherine ever did. She did not care when you dallied with other women, or even if you loved them. But I am not like Catherine! Whenever I hear that you have been with another, my heart is broken."

"Enough!" he said harshly. "I will hear no more of this, madam."

And when I stammered out more protestations, he rose and walked away. I remained on my knees, weeping. At the door he stopped, turned, stared down at me. For a moment my heart, and my hopes, lifted. "You have seduced me by witchcraft," he said. "I wish only to be free of you."

He was gone, and I collapsed, sobbing, upon the cold floor.

DURING THIS WRETCHED time, my only consolation was music. I had once made the acquaintance of Mark Smeaton, a commoner with an uncommon musical talent. Now it became his habit to visit me each afternoon in my chambers. There, in the presence of Nell, he played for me upon the clavichord, giving me some pleasure—perhaps the only pleasure of those dreary weeks when I had nothing to think about but my failure and the pale face of my young rival, Jane Seymour. I longed for a glimpse of my daughter, Elizabeth, and planned to visit her when I was stronger.

Music could do only so much to heal me. I was distraught. My best hope was my brother, who, like my father, was one of the most influential members of the privy chamber. If the Boleyns could only defeat the power of Cromwell, perhaps I still had a chance.

But it was too late. Cromwell had already begun to gather my personal enemies, together with those staunch supporters of the former queen and now of Mary, and even some of my disgruntled servants, all of whom were happy to condemn me. "There was never such a whore in all the realm," one of my ladies-in-waiting, Lady Wingfield, told the king, according to George.

My brother and I sat in the privy garden, where there was less chance of an eavesdropper, for we both believed ourselves surrounded by spies. The warm spring sunshine and birds twittering in the trees seemed an insult and only added to my sense of foreboding. "The king listens to all these rumors and reports, mostly from Cromwell, and he says nothing," George said quietly. "He no longer listens to me, or to our father." George hesitated before he asked, "What can you tell me of Mark Smeaton?"

To calm myself, I kept my hands busy with a piece of needlework, a book cover intended for Henry with our intertwined initials, *H & A*, embroidered upon it. "Mark Smeaton is a fine musician. He comes often to play for me. Surely you are not suggesting—?"

"I suggest nothing, dear sister. But others have. That same Lady Wingfield claims that Smeaton has visited not only your privy chamber but your bed-chamber as well, where he hides in a cupboard until you summon him to join you behind the bed-curtains."

"But it is a lie!" I cried, leaping to my feet and dropping my stitchery. "Nothing that you suggest has even a grain of truth to it! I have never been unfaithful to the king." Infuriated, I trampled the stitchery in the dirt. But even as I protested, I realized what was happening. The king would not simply have our marriage annulled and send me to rot in some country manor. He would have me accused of being unfaithful to him. Adultery against the king is treason, punishable by death.

*Death!* Did the king, my husband, mean to have me killed? Surely not! Surely not! I stared at the muddied piece of linen, the *H & A* ruined, realizing that *he surely would.* Faint with terror, I fell upon my knees and lifted my eyes to George. "Help me," I pleaded. "For God's sake, help me!"

"I cannot," he said, slowly shaking his head. Then he added grimly, "God help us both."

AT THE END OF APRIL, I learned that Cromwell, by order of King Henry, had begun an investigation of treason against the king. I scarcely dared imagine what this might mean. On the first of May, so undone and frightened that I could scarcely still my trembling hands, I attended a May Day joust with Henry and members of the court. I remember almost nothing of what transpired at the joust. Barely halfway through the events, the king abruptly summoned several of his friends and rode off without even a farewell, leaving me sitting alone and terrified of what might happen next. Later I was told that he claimed to have seen me drop a handkerchief, which he chose to believe was a signal I had given to a lover.

Within hours, three of Henry's closest friends—the men who had ridden off with him—were arrested: Henry Norris, William Brereton, and Francis Weston. So was the musician, Mark Smeaton. So—unbelievably—was my brother, George. All were accused of treason.

Had the king gone mad? Surely it was not simply his desire for a son that was behind this. Surely it was not simply his lust for a younger wife. Half mad with terror myself, I could only conclude that the king had taken leave of his senses and that Cromwell fueled the flames of his madness.

Nell stayed close by me during those last terrible hours, as I waited to learn if I, too, would be taken away. Distraught, I asked her to send for Elizabeth, my bright and winsome little daughter, who had at last been brought to Greenwich for a visit a fortnight before. When Nell carried her to me, I held the child tightly to my breast, bathing us both in tears.

The king's messenger appeared at my apartments.

At the sight of him, I began to tremble so violently that I nearly dropped my daughter. I tried to speak to him haughtily, but no words would come. The messenger's eyes were cold, his words even colder: I was to be arrested within the hour and tried for treason, "by order of His Majesty, the king."

"Take the child to the king," Nell urged me, as soon as the messenger had gone. "Let him look upon you both!"

I begged permission to stand outside the palace, beneath the windows of the king's privy chamber with the child in my arms, hoping the sight of us would open his heart once more. I knew that Henry was there; I was certain that he saw us, although he gave no sign. I stood there until the guards appeared and dragged me away. Elizabeth, my daughter, my last hope, was taken from me.

I WRITE THIS NOW from my chamber in the Tower, to which I was brought by barge on the second of May. On that day I was questioned by a tribunal headed by my uncle, the duke of Norfolk. My father was not present, for which I am grateful, for I could not have borne to have him point an accusing finger at me, as he did at my brother and the others. How could he do this to his own son? I know not, unless it was to save his own life. My uncle undid me from the start when he showed me a paper signed by Mark Smeaton, confessing that he had been my lover.

"But it is a lie!" I cried. "We were not lovers!

You forced this confession from him, so that you can unjustly condemn me!"

"Silence!" shouted my uncle Norfolk. "The accused is forbidden to speak!"

Then I was brought here, to the very chamber where I spent the night before my coronation. I am in the custody of the constable of the Tower, Sir William Kingston, and his wife. I try my best to retain my dignity, but I confess that my composure often deserts me, and I veer from wanton laughter to crushing tears in a matter of moments—a trial, I am sure, to him and Lady Kingston.

George was taken elsewhere in the Tower, charged with having been my lover. My own brother was condemned by the testimony of his jealous wife, who claimed that I bragged to her of sleeping with several men to ensure that I would conceive a male child! The others, too, were imprisoned here—Norris, Brereton, Weston. And poor Smeaton.

Four ladies have been sent to attend me, none of whom I would wish to spend even a pleasant hour with, let alone these horrible ones. Mistress Coffin, whom I know to be a spy, is assigned to report my every word to my jailer. Are they waiting for me to confess to amours with the accused men? *With my own brother?* For that they will wait a lifetime, for it is the invention of Cromwell, and I swear there is no truth to it.

But no one wants to hear the truth.

Despite my most devout prayers, the indictments

against me and the others were handed down on the tenth of May, charging me with engaging in carnal pleasure with the accused. There were even dates given for the occasions on which I supposedly lured them to my bed! The one that pained me most deeply was the charge against my brother. It was even suggested that George is the father of my daughter, Elizabeth! How could anyone believe such a thing?

The men were found guilty, without a shred of evidence, of conspiring the king's death. On the twelfth of May, the convicted men were condemned to die as traitors.

My trial took place on the fifteenth. I was allowed to offer no defense. Perhaps it would have made no difference if I had had the most skillful lawyers in the land to plead my case. I swore my innocence. I begged that I might be spared, allowed to live out the rest of my days in a nunnery, but my pleas went unheeded. I was found guilty and escorted from the courtroom by six guards whose axheads were turned toward me, a signal to the crowds waiting silently for a verdict that I was condemned to die.

Kingston tells me that Archbishop Cranmer has declared my marriage to Henry invalid—not because of the king's prior marriage to Catherine, but because of his affair with my sister, Mary. My daughter, Elizabeth, has been declared a bastard. I think often of the other Mary, Henry's daughter, and wonder what will become of her. I have told Lady Kingston that I now understand how deeply I have wronged my stepdaughter, and I would go to my death more easily if Princess Mary could find it in her heart to forgive me. I doubt that she will. If I were in her place, I could not.

AND SO MY STORY ENDS. Today I will die on the scaffold on Tower Green. I still cling to a fragile hope that my beloved husband, King Henry VIII, will reconsider—that my life will be spared. Surely he will not kill me, the mother of his daughter! His loving wife, his loyal queen! But that hope weakens with every passing hour. I have known the man, the lover, the husband, the king, and in truth I know in my heart that he will not change his mind. His only gesture of mercy has been to send for a swordsman from Calais whose work is known to be swift and more merciful than the axman's.

Soon it will be first light. Nell will help me dress in my gown of gray silk. My chaplain will come to hear my last confession and to spend with me my final hour on earth. I will swear again by all that is holy: I have never been unfaithful to the king, in thought, word, or deed. Perhaps I should confess to him what I now understand to be my greatest sin: Pride. That I desired too much, reached too high. Whether or not I confess that, the ultimate sin against God, the priest will absolve me of all sin and offer me the holy sacrament for the last time.

Two days ago, I watched as the five men accused and condemned with me—each one of them as innocent as I—were taken to Tower Hill, outside the walls of the Tower. There they were executed as traitors: hanged, drawn, quartered, beheaded.

Today my turn will come. I am very afraid. I can scarcely breathe.

I do not know how I will be able to walk those last steps to the scaffold. Will my legs support my weight? Who will walk with me? Will I swoon and be carried up the wooden steps, my head placed upon the block by someone else's hands? And who will be there to see me die? Will they make any sound? What of dear Nell? Will she be there? Will the king watch from some secret place? Will he hear the last cry wrung from my lips? What will he feel as the sword falls and my soul flies from my body? Will he then dress in yellow and dance with his new love? And my daughter, Elizabeth? What will become of her?

When I die today, it will not be the lowborn Lady Anne Boleyn, but noble Queen Anne, wife of King Henry VIII of England, who enters into eternal life. If I must die, then I will die boldly, as I have lived.

# *EPILOGUE*

Anne Boleyn was beheaded on Tower Green, within the walls of the Tower, on the nineteenth of May, 1536. Her body and severed head were later buried in a tomb in the Chapel of Saint Peter ad Vincula in the Tower of London.

The day after Anne's execution, King Henry was betrothed to Jane Seymour; they were wed ten days later. On the twelfth of October, 1537, Queen Jane gave birth to a healthy son, named Edward. Within two weeks Queen Jane was dead of childbed fever.

Henry VIII wed three more times before his death in 1547 but fathered no more children. His son, Edward, who inherited the throne, died in 1553 and was succeeded by Mary. After Mary's death in 1558, Anne Boleyn's daughter, Elizabeth, was crowned queen and ruled for forty-five years.